SINGE DAD ON TAP

CATHRYN FOX

ISBN Ebook: 978-1-989374-13-9
ISBN Print: 978-1-989374-14-6

SINGLE DAD ON TAP

Single Dad on Tap

1

___

OLIVIA

___

"Rain, rain go away."

I push open the heavy pub door, hold my palm out and lift my face to the dark sky. Any second now, those heavy clouds are going to open up and saturate the downtown streets of Boston. I only live three blocks away, but if I hurry, maybe I can make it before that happens. I snort. As if I have that kind of luck. Still, I have no choice but to hoof it on foot, so I tuck my apron into my backpack, step outside and let the pub door fall shut behind me.

"Here goes nothing."

I hit the sidewalk and start speed walking home. The jiggling of my ass might not be pretty, but I can't run. No, running and I, well... we're not friends. We never have been, which is why I've been curvy for as long as I can remember. I make it one block, almost halfway there, and I'm about to throw up a hallelujah when a bright flash zigzags across the sky, followed by rumbling thunder, and big fat rain drops.

"Well, hell."

I put my backpack over my head and pick up the pace. Maybe my father was right. Maybe I should take his advice and borrow a few bucks from my Stanford college fund to buy an old beater for rainy days like these. With my Dad's ill health, he doesn't drive anymore, but at least his trips to the hospital are less and less frequent.

I'm not one to ask others for things, and getting an Uber every now and then to take him to his appointments is a lot cheaper than owning a car. Not that we ever had to rely on an Uber. Jesse, the guy whose lived next door to me since we were kids, and owner of Burgers and Brews Pub where I work, has always been there to lend a helping hand. But he's a single dad, who works all hours running his own business. With those kinds of demands tugging at him, he doesn't need to be taking on my problems.

Speaking of my neighbor…

I turn my head as his vehicle slows next to me on the street. The rain-soaked window slides open, and a little sigh catches in my throat when my gaze lands on his handsome face. I resist the urge to smooth my hand over my wet hair and primp like a love-struck teenager. The effort would be futile. We're friends, and he'd never see me as anything more.

"Get in," he says, and I nod. I step off the curb and my foot lands in a deep puddle. Well, isn't my day just getting better and better. I curse under my breath as he leans over to open the door for me and I slide into the passenger seat. I set my wet backpack on the floor beside my drenched shoe, and push my hair from my face.

"I'm getting your car all wet."

He shrugs and casts me a fast glance. My heart wobbles, the way it always does when I become the sole focus of his attention. "It's just a car."

With so much responsibility on this man's shoulders, I have no idea how he remains so laid back and easygoing. But I guess that's what makes him a great bar owner/bartender. I've known him long enough to know he's given up a lot to take over the pub after his parents died years ago, when his son was less than a year old. Burgers and Brews was their pride and joy—it's been in the family for generations—and Jesse is loyal to a fault, giving up his dreams so he could keep theirs alive. It's commendable, yet I'm not sure that's what they wanted for him. Not that I could tell him that. It's not really my business. But I hate that the man threw his dreams away.

He glances over his shoulder to check for traffic. "You should have called me."

"It's your day off, Jesse. Besides, I'm a big girl. A little rain doesn't hurt me. I'm not made of sugar, you know." I peer into the back seat. "Hey Lucas," I say. "How are you?"

Lucas doesn't acknowledge me. He rarely does and I've gotten used to his behavior over the years. With high-functioning autism, he has trouble engaging socially. I wait for an answer, but sweet little Lucas, all of five years old, continues to stare at the dinosaur book in his hand.

"Lucas," Jesse says, his voice deep. "Olivia is talking to you." Lucas lifts his head and stares at his dad in the rearview mirror. "Answer her, please."

"I'm good," he says, and goes back to his book.

"I think he's going to grow up to be a writer," I say. "Or a dinosaur." Jesse flashes me a smile. The love he has for his son fills his eyes and spills onto his handsome face. My God, does he have to be so damn good looking? What did I do in a past lifetime to live next to the hottest guy on the planet—one who had a baby with my best friend and has never seen me as anything more than the chubby girl next door? He might be every girl's type, but I've come to terms with the fact that I'm not his.

"He does love books," he says.

I grin. "He takes after his dad." The smile falls from his face and I mentally curse myself. Shit, he's probably thinking about how he's glad Lucas doesn't take after his mom, Kylie. She up and left when Lucas was closing in on two years old—after his diagnosis. She'd been back and forth a few times, always causing chaos in their lives, but no one has heard from her in the last year. She just ghosted us all.

Kylie and I became instant friends when she moved here with her mother and stepdad in tenth grade. She was loud, fun and vivacious, and I never knew why she wanted to be friends with the nerdy bookworm. There were times I thought it was to get closer to Jesse, but she didn't need me for that. She was like a damn glowstick and attracted attention everywhere she went. Top that off with a rich stepfather who tried to buy her affection, and in my books, she had it all. I was happy for her, though. I'm just not happy with the way things worked out between her and Jesse. I want him to be happy.

"How was work?" Jesse asks, changing the subject.

"Busy. People have nothing to do but hang out, play pool and drink beer with this wet weather. Plus, tonight is paint night." I chuckle. "People are coming in early to grab a bite to eat beforehand. Dad is there now, eating and drinking and guarding the best seat in the house."

He chuckles. "God forbid anyone who tries to steal Jack's seat at the front of the class." He casts me a quick glance, that dimple on his right cheek toying viciously with my libido. "Like father, like daughter."

I whack him, and wish I hadn't. When my hand hits his taut stomach muscles, ribbons of need reverberate through me, hitting all my girly spots. "I'm not that bad," I say. It's a lie. I am. I'm a nerd, the girl who sits at the front of the class, and take copious amounts of notes. It's not a bad thing, though. All my hard work has paid off, and come September, I'll be attending Stanford's Human Resource Management master's program. I want to be a human resource consultant and help organizations, plus moving Dad to a warmer climate will be so much better for his rheumatoid arthritis. The cold and damp here in Boston is very hard on him.

Jesse pulls into my driveway and I snatch up my wet backpack. "Thanks. I owe you one."

"Nah, you've been doing so much at the pub, I owe you one."

"Happy to help." He's been such a good friend, always been there for me, and I like being there for him, too.

"Okay, go," he says, glancing out the front window as the rain slows, like it's taunting me, daring me to step from the vehicle. "Try to run between the drops."

I laugh, jump from the car and run. As I hurry up my driveaway, another cloud bursts open right over my head and drenches me. Yelping, I dash up the three steps to the old bungalow I've lived in my entire life, even when attending Boston University.

I turn and wave to Jesse and Lucas when I reach the covered porch. Jesse backs out of my driveway and pulls into his beside mine as I search my backpack. Where the hell is my key? I put it in there this morning. I specifically remember doing it. I crouch and empty the contents of my bag onto the welcome mat.

"Where the heck is it?"

The wind picks up, and a chill goes through me. I could call Dad, but I don't want him walking home in this, and I don't want him to lose his seat. I give a resigned sigh, and spot Jesse and Lucas heading inside their home. He usually has a spare key but last week, I had to get it from him when I couldn't find mine—and of course I forgot to give it back. This is becoming a bit of a habit. I guess I'll have to take shelter at their place and wait out the storm. Dad's old friend Heidi, who he paints, plays bingo and goes to garage sales with, will drive Dad home after they finish painting, until then...

I dash down the stairs and run to the neighboring house. I rap on the door and a few seconds later it swings open.

"What's up?" Jesse asks, frowning as he takes in the wet mess that is me. "I thought you were going to run between the drops."

I point upward. "There was a big-ass cloud itching for a fight."

"It obviously won." His gaze drops, and I put my backpack in front of my soaked chest—not that he was ogling me or anything. He wasn't. But I look like I just came from a wet T-shirt contest and don't want him to think I'm flaunting or flirting or anything. Not that I'm good at either one of those things.

"I can't find my key."

"Again?"

"I know."

He widens the door. "Then come on in."

I step inside and a cold shiver goes through me as he swings the door shut. "It's so weird. I know I put it in my bag."

He frowns. "You don't think someone at the pub is going into your bag, do you?"

"I can't imagine. It was in my locker in your office." I shake my head. "Maybe I just forgot. My days are all running together."

"That's because you've been working too hard."

He's not wrong. I've been working extra hours to save for Stanford. Dad gave up work at the paper when he was diagnosed with respiratory disease, and is living on a pension. He's offered to help but I'm not taking his retirement money, and this is something I want to do on my own. Besides, I don't mind helping Jesse out and lightening his load.

"Things should slow down tomorrow after the firefighters' pancake breakfast," I say.

"I'll be there to help out first thing, too." Gorgeous blue eyes lock on mine as he steps closer and runs his hands up and down my arms to create heat with friction. He's a smart guy, one of the smartest I know, but he has no idea what his touch and close proximity do to me. Maybe I should be in theater instead of human resources. I've gotten so used to acting like his mere presence does nothing to me. Truthfully, I pride myself on my honesty, except for when it comes to my feelings for this man.

"Right now, we need to get you out of those wet clothes," he says.

Oh God.

As my mind envisions exactly how I'd like to remove them, my body warms all over.

Get it together, Olivia.

I might have had the hots for him since I was a teen, but he doesn't think about me like that. No, to him, I'm the girl next door, his buddy, friend-zoned forever. No way would I ever try something and risk rejection or awkwardness between us. Having him in my life as a friend is better than not having him at all. Not to mention his ex was my best friend.

"I'm just getting Lucas something to eat and settled. Why don't you grab some clothes from my dresser and jump into a hot shower."

I peer around his shoulders and spot Lucas at the kitchen table. "Are you sure I'm not interrupting?" Routine is very important to Lucas, and I don't want to do anything to disrupt it.

"Of course not."

Even if I was in his way, cutting into his precious time

with his son, and messing with their routines, he'd never turn me away. He's seriously one of the nicest guys I know.

My teeth chatter when I say, "That sounds perfect, actually."

"Head on up. Lucas is just having a snack."

I nod and he turns sideways to clear the path. I walk past him in the narrow entranceway, my body brushing his. It's all I can do to swallow a moan as I bump his hard muscles and revel in the way his heat wraps around me.

I dart up the stairs and walk to his room. During college, he lived in an apartment, but after his parents passed away, he moved into their home to singlehandedly raise his son. I step into his bedroom and take a breath, my heart somewhere around the vicinity of my throat.

It's been a while since I've been in here, and the once messy bedroom, clothes on the floor, and football trophies everywhere, is now clean and stark, giving an unlived-in feeling. I understand he has to keep his space clean and minimal for his son's sake—everything in order helps Lucas keep a calmness in his chaotic life. Jesse does an amazing job caring for his son, but it does beg the question, who the hell is caring for him? From the looks of his room, this man isn't living, he's simply going through the motions of getting from one day to the next. He needs more, he needs something for himself. That much I know. But he hasn't been with anyone since Kylie. I hate that she bolted and broke his heart.

Pushing those sad thoughts down, I step up to his dresser. My hand goes to my stomach as I take in the silver frame showcasing a picture of father and son. Emptiness takes up residence inside of me. Two years ago, the doctors told me my chances of conceiving were slim to none. Thanks to my painful endometriosis, and the severe scarring on my tubes, movement of egg and sperm through the tube is near impossible. If I ever get married, it would have to be to a guy who is okay with no kids. Not that I see marriage in my future. I have to get over the crush on the man whose room I'm in before I can move on.

I tug open Jesse's dresser and find a pair of sweats and a big T-shirt. I glance over my shoulder to make sure the coast is clear before I bring them to my nose and inhale his fabric softener. Pathetic, I know.

God, I am such a creeper.

Footsteps sound on the stairs, followed by Jesse's voice as I make my way to the main bathroom and shut the door behind me. I strip off, not an easy chore when my jeans are soaking wet. I finally get undressed and hop into the shower, turning the spray to super-hot. I revel in the heat and lather my body with Jesse's body wash. Now I'm going to smell like him all night, which probably isn't a good thing. No, it will just have my thoughts going in a direction they have no right going.

Once I'm warm and clean, I step from the shower and reach for a towel. Before I can get my hands on it, the bathroom door flings open and hits the wall with a thud.

"Jesus," I yelp, and nearly slip on the floor.

Jesse comes racing in behind Lucas, yelling at him to stop, but alas, it's too late. My hot neighbor comes to an abrupt halt, his eyes wide and horrified as he stands behind his son, gaping at my nakedness.

Dear ground, please open up and swallow me whole.

He grabs Lucas by the shoulders and turns him around, and gentleman that he is, he pinches his eyes shut.

"Sorry," he says quickly. "I don't think he realized you were in here and he got away before I could stop him."

I snatch the towel and wrap it around my body. "It's okay," I say, even though I'm completely and utterly mortified. "It was an accident."

With his eyes still closed, he points. "There's a towel."

"Yeah, I know." Clearly this man does *not* want to see me naked. "I'm covered."

He peels one eye open, and his gaze drops to take in the fluffy blue towel tied around me. Relief washes through him and his shoulders relax.

"I uh…I'll let you get dressed," he says. "I'm going to read Lucas a story and get him settled in. Why don't you meet me downstairs when you're done."

"Sure," I say, except if I get there first, I plan to run all the way to Canada.

2

JESSE

Holy Mother of Hotness!

I tug on my hair—and adjust my pants—as I pull the bathroom door shut and take Lucas back to his bedroom. I always knew Olivia was well built and curvy, but seeing her without clothes, getting a up close and personal view of all her gorgeous nakedness is not something a man can erase from his memory—ever. The gentleman in me forced me to close my eyes, but my traitorous cock however, encouraged me to stand there and drink her in. My God, those breasts, those sweet pink nipples...

Stop!

Do *not* think about her like that.

Truth be told, it's not the first time I've noticed her innocent sexuality. But as a girl who is completely career-driven, her sights set on Stanford, she's completely oblivious to the men around her, blind to what others see in her, and how she commands the attention of a room the second she walks in. I've caught more than one guy at the bar eyeing her with want. But she gives off unattainable vibes, whether she realizes it or not. Is she holding out for someone in particular?

I'm not sure, but Christ, when she sashays around in those form-fitting jeans, and a tight T-shirt that displays ample breasts ...well, my friends, that's what fantasies are made of. At least mine are. Yeah, it's true. I've jacked off a few times with her on my brain. But it's wrong. I can't think of my friend like that—a girl I've known and lived beside forever—and she doesn't think about me like that. In fact, when her best friend Kylie hit on me in college, it was Olivia who encouraged me to go for it.

We step into Lucas' room and I work to wipe the image from my brain, although I'm afraid it just may be burned into my retinas forever now. How I'm going to meet her downstairs and play it cool is beyond me, but I have to. No matter what, I can't start anything with Olivia. Our lives are on different paths, and she's headed to California for school in a few months. She has dreams to fulfil, and she'd only come to resent anything or anyone who tampered with her ambitions.

"Okay buddy, which book do you want tonight?"

Lucas growls, and holds his hands up. "Dinosaurs."

"Of course," I say and laugh. My boy has an obsession with prehistoric animals. "Which one?"

He runs to his massive bookcase and grabs one of the many books on dinosaurs. "This one."

I tug his sheets down and tap the bed, but I'm momentarily distracted when the bathroom door opens and the stairs creak.

Be cool, dude.

Lucas jumps into bed, and I pull the sheets up. I crack the book and for the next thirty minutes I read it to him numerous times until his lids grow heavy. I set the book down, and my heart pinches as I kiss him goodnight.

It's not right that he's growing up without a mom, and on one hand I'm angry that Kylie just up and left—causing chaos in our life whenever she returned home for a visit—yet on the other, she had dreams she wanted to fulfill in Hollywood. She grew to resent us both, and when I took over the bar instead of going to med school, she took off for bigger and better things. I guess we just weren't enough, and the way I see it, two is better than three, if that third person harbors resentment. While I hate that Lucas is motherless, he does have my grandmother, and Olivia. They both adore him. I hope that's enough for him because right now, I'm not interested in bringing another woman into our lives. If Kylie ever materializes again, I'd have to think long and hard on whether I'd even let her see Lucas again, especially if she's just going to blow in and blow out again. Right now, my focus is keeping my son happy and healthy and turmoil free, and keeping my business running, and that's all I need.

The front door creaks open and I slip from Lucas' room and descend the stairs two at a time. I spot Olivia standing on the stoop with her palm up.

"Going somewhere?"

She turns, her eyes wide. "You startled me."

The second I see her vivacious body in my clothes, my dick swells. I take one breath and then another, and resist the urge to push her up against the wall and bury myself in her.

Man, I need to get out more often.

"Sorry, didn't mean to frighten you."

Her eyes narrow as I continued to stand there and take in her body. In a self-conscious gesture, she folds her arms across her chest.

"Is something wrong?" she asks.

Oh, yeah, something is definitely wrong. Because I shouldn't be wanting her like this.

I scrub the scruff on my face. "No, it's just strange seeing you in my clothes. Caught me off guard is all."

"I've been in your clothes before. Remember when I was here for your birthday and spilled juice all over my dress?"

"Yeah, but you were eight, and we were almost the same size then."

She lifts her arms and lets them flop to her sides. "Kind of big now, huh?"

"Yeah," I say, as I think about climbing in there with her. *Don't make this awkward, dude.*

"I put my clothes in your dryer. I hope you don't mind."

"Not at all."

She crinkles her cute little nose. "They should be ready soon and I can get out of these."

"No hurry," I say, enjoying the view far too much. "Come on. Your dad won't be back for a bit, so let's hang out."

"It's been a long time since we just hung out," she says.

She's right. It's been a long time since it was just the two of us. As kids, our dads were great friends—she lost her mom when she was small—and my mom took her under her wing. When they died, the loss was hard for her too. But she hung out here a lot, and even though she was a couple of years younger, we always got along. By the time high school hit, we both went off and did our own thing, and in my last year of college, I hooked up with her best friend, and that's what brought us back together again. Olivia was there all through Kylie's pregnancy, and often times it was just her and me when Kylie was resting or out with her parents, who had no trouble showing their disappointment when I took over the bar instead of going to med school. I guess if I didn't make more of myself, I wasn't good enough for their daughter.

"Movie and ice cream?" I ask.

She grins. "Only my favorite way to wind down."

"I know." I pick up the remote and hand it to her. "Find us something. I'll grab the ice cream."

She stifles a yawn as she plops down on the sofa and tucks her legs in behind her. Damn she looks good enough to eat. I stare for a moment, and she angles her head.

"Jesse? Is everything...okay?"

"Yeah, just ah, things on my mind." Things I have no right to be thinking about. "Ice cream is on the way."

I dash to the kitchen, grab the small tub of ice cream from the freezer and momentarily think about shoving the tub down my pants. I need to cool the fuck off. Two spoons in one hand, the tub in the other, I step back into the living room to find her, legs stretched out, on the sofa. She tugs them back and sits up.

"Rocky Road. Mmm, my favorite." She licks her lips and ah, yeah, that messes with my ability to think with clarity.

I gesture toward the TV. "What did you find?"

"A romantic comedy."

I groan. "Seriously. We can't watch something with car chases and buildings blowing up?"

"No," she says with a tip of her chin. "You need to expand your horizons."

She turns up the volume. "How many times have you seen this one?" I ask as Jennifer Lopez gets her shoe stuck in a grate.

"Hush," she says and digs her spoon into the ice cream. My heart beats a little faster as she slides the spoon into her mouth and makes a sexy bedroom noise that teases my cock. Okay, maybe ice cream was a bad idea.

"Good, huh?" I ask. Shit, was that my voice?

"Delicious."

As I consider something else I'd like to see sliding between her lips, she settles against me and digs her spoon in again. Since I'm not a total masochist, I turn my focus to the TV. She moans again and my gaze slides her way. Yeah, okay maybe I am.

We go silent for a long time, and polish off the ice cream as the movie comes to an end. A small sigh escapes her lips.

"What?" I ask.

"I love the way he looks at her."

I chuckle, and take in the wistful look spreading across her pretty face. "You're a true romantic at heart, aren't you?"

She shrugs. "Maybe." She gives a heavy sigh. "I wish a guy would look at me like that," she says quietly, to herself—like I wasn't meant to hear it. Oh, but I did hear it.

"Yeah?" I ask. "Anyone in particular?"

As if she said too much, her eyes widen and she inches away, pressing her back against the arm of the sofa.

She shakes her head fast and blurts out, "What? No." Her forceful protest makes me think she's not telling the truth.

I grab her legs and put them on my lap. It's not something I haven't done before, but this time, and I can't explain why, it feels more...intimate. "So, you *do* like someone. What's his name?"

"It's nothing. No one," she says, but I'm not about to let it go. I care about her, and I'd love to see her find the love of her life, a guy who will treat her the way she deserves to be treated.

"Come on, you can tell me," I say, and push down the strange niggling feeling of jealousy.

She makes a move to sit up, but I squeeze her legs and hold her down. She takes a fast breath, a hint of color crawling up her neck. Whoa. Either she likes it when I restrain her, or she really doesn't want to talk about this.

Do not think about restraining her, dude.

Do not think about tying her down and having your way with her.

Dammit, I'm thinking about it.

"It's nothing...no one," she says again, with a dismissive wave of her hand this time. "Can we please talk about something else."

"Nope," I tease. "I want to know all about lover boy."

She rolls her eyes so hard it nearly gives me a headache. "Lover boy? Are you twelve?"

"Sometimes," I joke. I'm well past puberty, but my dirty thoughts aren't.

"Look there's nothing to tell. I'm invisible to him."

I open my mouth, but she turns her head when a car door slams next door. She tugs her legs away and jumps up. "Looks like Dad is home."

I stand and walk her to the door as she slides her feet into her damp work shoes. "Thanks for letting me hang out."

"Aren't you forgetting something?" That sexy pink color moves into her cheeks, as I lean toward her. Unable to help myself, I run the hem of her T-shirt between my thumb and finger. My knuckles brush warm, soft skin, and my throat dries. I've been able to stifle my want for this woman for a long time, but seeing her naked, all that beautiful creamy skin, must have snapped the last thread holding me together.

Stop flirting, dude. She is not the girl for you.

She blinks rapidly, and furrows her brow. "No, what?"

"You're still in my clothes."

Her head jerks up. "Oh right. I'll change."

"Don't worry about it." I casually roll one shoulder. "You can get your clothes tomorrow."

"Oh, okay," she says and looks like she's about to bolt. Not that I blame her, I'm very close to crossing a line here, and she obviously doesn't want that.

"One more thing."

She grips the doorknob tighter. "What?"

"If you really want the guy, I say go for it. Make him notice you."

3

OLIVIA

Make him notice you.

As I tie my apron around my waist, Jesse's parting words from last night continue to ping around in my lust-rattled brain. It's all I could think about in bed. That, and the way his knuckles brushed my stomach when he ran the cotton T-shirt I was wearing between his fingers. Did something happen between us last night, or am I just imagining things? I tossed that question around until the wee hours of the morning, which is why I'm standing here trying to stifle a yawn as the firetrucks pull into the pub's parking lot.

Today, the firefighters will be giving demonstrations to the community. Burgers and Brews will be providing the pancakes, and donating all the profits. The whole event is to raise funds for the hospital's burn unit. It was something Jesse's family started years ago, and I'm happy to see my boss carrying on with the very important cause.

"Ooh, I do love a hot firefighter," Tara says as she steps up next to me and curls a long strand of hair around her finger. Tara is a few years older than me. She's gorgeous, funny and quick, and I'm not sure what her story is, but she's definitely anti-marriage. *Why eat the cake when you can sample different icing every weekend?* Her words, not mine.

"Who doesn't," I tease. Yeah, after catching me staring at Jesse a time or two, it's better for her to think I have the hots for one of the firefighters. I don't want anyone at the pub getting the wrong idea—or rather, the right idea. The last thing I want is for rumors to spread and threaten the long-standing friendship we have.

"Which one do you like?"

"I think you mean, which one don't I like," I tease, and it brings on a laugh.

Colin, who grew up two blocks over, climbs from the cab of the truck. He's a nice guy, and I like talking to him. A gorgeous woman dressed in short shorts and a tank top walks up to him and a smile spreads across his face. I watch the exchange; study the way the woman is flirting with him. I'd probably look like a chimpanzee jacked on Red Bull if I moved my hips and arms like that. But this woman is pulling it off and it seems like Colin appreciates her efforts.

"Oh my God," Tara says, her eyes going wide. "You like Colin."

"Of course, I like—"

My words die on my tongue when Jesse steps up to us. He puts his mouth near my ear and says, "Looks like your secret is out."

Oh, crap. I should correct him—tell him I like Colin as a friend only—but maybe letting him think I have the hots for the hot firefighter is better than him figuring who I'm really into.

I take in Jesse's grin as he hands me a paper cup filled to the rim with coffee. He's always so thoughtful, such a gentleman. Is it wrong of me to wish he wasn't always a nice guy? To wish he'd take me in the back room, tear my clothes from my body and ravish me? Those erotic images instantly heat me up, and deep between my legs, my clit quivers.

Oh boy!

"Thanks," I say gratefully and take a much-needed sip, wishing it was ice water and I could pour it over my head.

"You looked like you could use a cup." His eyes narrow, take me in, and I try not to fidget under his inspection. "Everything okay?"

"Fine," I lie. "Just a bit tired today. The rain pounding on my window kept me up."

"You should go for it," Tara says and my gaze jerks to hers.

"Go for what?" I blurt out quickly. God, is my attraction to Jesse that obvious?

She flips her hand over. "Go for Colin."

"Oh," I say, my head bobbing. "Right."

She arches a manicured brow. "Who did you think I meant?"

"Colin. I thought you meant Colin." The truth is I'm a wallflower, a book nerd. Even if I did like Colin, I'm not the kind of girl a popular guy like him would go for. "I'd have to be on fire for him to notice me," I say, putting an end to the conversation. I'm about to walk away when Tara grabs my arm and produces a lighter.

"Here you go," she says with a grin.

"Ah, she's not setting herself on fire, Tara," Jesse says.

"No, but maybe she could start a small fire in her backyard, or better yet, her bedroom. Then once she has him there, they can set the sheets on fire, if you know what I mean."

"We all know what you mean." Jesse crosses his arms and shakes his head at the ludicrous suggestion. "And she's not doing any of that. Fires can easily get out of hand. It's a bad idea."

"Bad ideas." She breathes deep and a wistful look comes over her as she exhaled. "Don't you just love them."

"No, I don't, and that's not how to get any guy's attention."

He's right. Nothing good can come from a bad idea. My gaze goes back and forth between the two of them as they discuss my lack of love life.

"I'm right here," I say. "I can hear you both." I take another big sip of my coffee.

Ignoring me, Tara frowns at Jesse. "Why are you cock-blocking, Boss? You want her for yourself or something?"

I nearly choke on my coffee as Jesse's head rears back.

"Okay, enough," I say. "I'm not setting anything, or anyone, on fire, and I'm not his type anyway, so can we all please just get back to work. I have a million pancakes to make."

"That's crazy. You're hot, Olivia. You're every guy's type." While I appreciate her vote of confidence, I'm smart enough to know I'm not. Guys like thin girls, and I've been through enough fad diets to know I'll never be gracing any magazine cover. Not that I want to. Men might not notice me, but over the years, I've come to accept my curves. I haven't learned to love them yet, but they're here to stay, so hopefully one day, we'll be best friends. No one has filled that role since Kylie left.

Tara snaps her finger and looks me up and down. "Get it, girl."

"What I'm getting is a headache." I'm about to step away when Tara's hand on my arm stops me.

"And that's why you need to get laid." She glances at Jesse. "And I know you agree, Jesse."

"I...what?" He swallows. "I never said that."

Tara stares him down. "You never *not* said that, either."

Is this conversation really happening? "Okay, now I really do have a headache."

"Wait," Tara says, "I got it. I know how to get him to notice you without this." She flicks the lighter before shoving it back into her pocket.

"I'm not—"

"I know guys." She winks at me. "I know how they think."

"Really now?" Jesse asks, and raises a skeptical brow. "This I want to hear."

"Yeah, you guys are easy. So, here's what you need to do, Olivia." She leans into me conspiratorially. "Show him you're the hottest girl in town. More than friendship material."

My jaw drops open. "Uh..." I mumble, not even knowing what to say to that.

She shrugs easily. "Guys want what other guys have." Jesse opens his mouth, but she reaches over and pinches his lips shut. "I suggest you and Jesse pretend you're an item." She chuckles. "He's the hottest ticket in town, you know, right?"

Oh, I know, but I don't say that.

"I don't think—" Jesse tries to say between his pinched lips.

"That's right, guys don't *think*," Tara says. "You two pretend you're an item. Laugh, flirt, kiss in public, and act like happy lovers. Once Colin sees you in Jesse's arms, believe me, he'll take notice and it will open up all kinds of possibilities for you."

"Why would he ask me out if I'm with someone else?" I toy with the plastic lid on my coffee cup, needing something to do with my restless hands. "I don't get it."

She stares at me like I might have a tumor, then shakes her head. "Don't you see? Being with Jesse is just to get him to notice you. Then you guys can stage a breakup." She lets go of Jesse's lips. "I know you want to help her out, Boss. I mean, you want her to find someone as much as I do, and Colin is one hell of a catch if you ask me."

One, no one is asking her, and two, when she phrases it like that, it leaves Jesse no back door to escape this insane plan. He's a good guy. The best guy I know, and he'd do anything for those he cares about. But no way would I let him do this, and honestly, I can't imagine he'd agree anyway.

I open my mouth to give him an out, when he blurts out, "I'll do it."

My jaw falls open, and I stare at him like *he's* the one with the brain tumor. "You can't be serious."

He shrugs. "It worked in that romantic comedy you made me watch last night."

"That's not how real life works, Jesse." Real life is messy, and complicated, and I'm not about to play with anyone's emotions—mainly mine. My God, if I had to pretend to be Jesse's girl, have him touch me, show public displays of affection, it would be emotional suicide at best.

"Well we'll never know if we don't try, right?" he says.

I angle my head, spot Colin coming our way. Tara makes a squealing sound. "Here he comes."

I wince at the high pitch in her voice and before I even realize what's happening, Jesse slides his arm around my waist and tugs me to him. My body meshes with his, and shivers of need zing through me. I pray to God he doesn't feel it. His Caribbean blue eyes lock on mine as his head dips, his lips closing over mine.

Dear God, what is going on here?

I'm not sure, and my brain is releasing so many endorphins, I'm not able to think about it with any sort of intelligence. Nope, all I'm able to do is revel in the sweetness of his mouth, the softness of his lips, and the small moan climbing out of his throat. Here I thought I was good at acting. This man could win an Oscar for this performance.

From the corner of my eye, I briefly catch Colin cast a glance our way as he walks past and heads inside the pub. Jesse's hands tighten around my back, and mine slide to his shoulders, taking pleasure in his muscles.

What the hell am I doing?

Tara's chuckle snaps some sense back into me. I break away, and pray to God I don't look or sound as breathless as I feel.

Tara grins. "Wow, for a second there, I didn't think you two were pretending."

I touch my tingling lips, and struggle to form a coherent sentence. "Of course we were."

"Yeah, yeah we were," Jesse adds, his chest rising and falling rapidly.

I put a shaky hand on my hip. "Jesse and I are friends, Tara, and this was *your* ludicrous idea."

"Ludicrous? I think not." She jerks her thumb over her shoulder. "Did you see the way Colin was looking at you?"

Not really, I was too busy kissing Jesse.

"Yeah, he was looking," I say. "I don't think..." I turn to Jesse. This is such a bad idea, and bad ideas are not good, right? He probably realizes that now, too. I expect to find him edgy, unsure, but no, he's swiping his tongue over his bottom lip like he's savoring the taste of me. What the ever-loving hell is going on? Either I'm being punked, or I'm having some strange sex dream about my neighbor—again.

Tara grins. "This is so going to work." She turns from me, and I swear to God I hear her mumble something about Jack being right.

"What was my father right about?" I ask. They better not have been discussing my love life.

"What?" she spins back around. "I never said anything about your father."

"I'm pretty sure you did."

"Oh, I said, Colin was jacked." She lifts her arms, and showcases her biceps. "He's so big and muscular. I can see why you like him." She winks. "Rumor has it the hot firefighter is great at rescuing kitties." She does air quotes around the word kitties.

"I don't have a…" I stop, and groan when my brain catches on to what she's really saying. "Oh my God, Tara."

"And don't worry, your secret is safe with me. I won't let anyone know you're…" She pauses to put her fingers in the air before adding, "pretending."

"Why did you just do air quotes around pretending?" I ask.

She blinks innocently. "Oh, no reason."

"Time to get back to work, Tara," Jesse says as he shakes his head.

"Okeydokey." She flashes us a bright smile before disappearing inside, leaving Jesse and me standing there.

A new kind of energy arcs between us, and his knuckles brush mine. "Hey," he says. "I hope that was okay. I mean, I was just trying to help out."

"You don't have to do this, you know," I tell him, working to calm my racing heart.

"I know. Maybe I want to."

"I feel like a damn charity case."

"You're not. Far from it. I think Tara might be on to something, actually. Colin really was taking notice."

My God, what have I gotten myself in to here?

"We can't let people think—"

Before I can finish, Colin steps outside, and Jesse pulls me to him again. His lips find mine, and I whimper as he kisses me. This time his tongue slides inside, soft and leisurely at first, but then he deepens the kiss, exploring the depths of me.

My God, I like this. I like it a lot.

But pretending we're a couple to get a guy I like only as a friend to notice me is insane.

Insanely delicious.

Nevertheless, I'm a smart girl and giving up these hot kisses would be foolish, right? Especially when I've been dreaming about them forever and they're so damn perfect. Maybe for the next couple of weeks before I head out west, we could keep on making out in public. Maybe I could simply enjoy this intimacy between us, and maybe, just maybe, it will help me get Jesse out of my system once and for all, and when I move away, I can start fresh. And hey, maybe this is what Jesse needs to. Something to shake up his world, and get him living again. Yeah, maybe I'm doing this for him more than I'm doing it for myself.

Maybe I do have a brain tumor.

His lips leave mine, and I can barely breathe as he glances over his shoulder to watch Colin move toward his fire truck. "Women really have a thing for firefighters huh?"

True. Although some have a thing for the boy next door.

"Yeah, I guess." I narrow my eyes. "Why would you do this, Jesse? What's in it for you?"

He opens his mouth, then closes it again. He glances down, like he's in deep thought and when his eyes meet mine again, he says, "I get to help out a friend."

Why do I get the sense he was going to say something entirely different?

"Too bad the sun is shining today," Tara says, coming out with pitchers of drinking water for the firefighters. "We could have turned this into a wet T-shirt contest. Now that would have raised some serious bucks."

Jesse shakes his head. "This is a family event, Tara."

"Well, I'm just saying. It might not be a bad fund-raising event some evening."

"Count me out," I say, and when I turn back to Jesse, his

gaze has dropped to my breasts. Why do I get the feeling he likes what he sees?

"Yeah, I think she'd win too, Boss," Tara says, and my head jerks up.

"I didn't mean...I'm not..." Jesse says, stumbling over his words, but there is no denying he was checking me out. Yeah, clearly this man isn't getting out enough and has to start dating again. Maybe pretending to be my guy will make him realize he does need a woman in his life. That thought almost makes me snort. What kind of woman wants to stir the libido of a guy she's crazy about, so he can find himself a new woman? A crazy one! Yeah, that's me. Next time, though, I need to help him pick someone who will stick around, and care about him and his son as much as I do.

JESSE

Apparently, I *am* a masochist.

I have no idea why I kissed her, or why I agreed to this ridiculous plan. Okay, maybe that's a fucking lie. Maybe I do know, and it's because I've been dying to press my mouth to hers, taste her sweetness, and feel her lush body meshed up against mine, even if it was for show. I'd been able to bury those wants, but seeing her naked was like a catalyst. The sight of those sexy curves set off a nuclear explosion inside my body, awakening parts of me that had been dormant for far too long. Now I'm on fire—for her—and there doesn't seem to be anything I can do about it.

This is so fucked.

I shouldn't want my friend like this and when it comes right down to it, she's into Colin, not me, and that's a good thing. A damn good thing. There can be no future for us— not that either of us want that. As long as I keep our public displays of affection, well...public, I should be okay. This is about helping her wake Colin the fuck up, not about my cock.

Yeah, I've got this.

"I'd better get at those pancakes," she says, her soft, low voice sliding over my skin and massaging my thickening dick. Christ.

"Yeah, I, uh…I'll be right in to help." I gesture with a nod. "I need to check with the guys to make sure they have everything for the demonstrations."

I catch Colin chatting it up with some pretty brunette. Olivia and Colin have been friends for a long time. Since childhood. We all have, in fact. But he's a player, out to bed as many women as he can. What I do know, however, is that when a guy meets the right girl, it can change him. I've seen it firsthand with many of my friends. I wouldn't quite say Kylie changed me. Yeah, I might have been a bit of a player, but when I'm with a woman, I'm monogamous. We were only together for a few months when she got pregnant, but I wanted to do the right thing and marry her. She up and left before that ever happened.

"I should go," Olivia says, bringing me back to the present. She darts away and I turn to Tara, who's grinning at me like she knows something I don't. But she's wrong. That kiss was more than it should have been, and yeah, I know that too.

Maybe I don't got this.

"I'll take those over," I say, and take the two big pitchers from her hands.

"Whatever you say, Boss."

I walk over to the firefighters, and check to see if they need anything. I'm about to head back inside when Colin nudges me.

"You and Olivia, huh?" He smirks at me, and glances past my shoulders like he's searching for her.

"Yeah, me and Olivia."

He tugs off his helmet and wipes his brow with the back of his arm. "How long as that been going on?"

"Kind of took me by surprise," I say.

He nods and tugs his helmet back on. "I always thought you two were good together."

What the hell? Really?

"Yeah, well, it's nothing serious."

"No?" he asks with hope and interest lighting his eyes, and before I realize what I'm doing, my fingers curl. I like Colin. I do. He's a nice guy, but he has a wicked reputation with the ladies. Olivia might want him, but the last thing I want is for him to hurt her. If I'm setting her up for disaster, I'd never forgive myself. "So you two are just messing around?"

"Something like that."

He nods, his brow furrowed in thought. "Hmm."

"What?"

"I don't know. I guess she never seemed like the type. She's different, you know. Growing up, she was always so quiet. She didn't party with us, or go to the football games. I just never thought..."

Shit. I don't like this. Not one bit at all.

"Yeah, well she's all grown up now."

A crooked grin curls the corner of his mouth. "I'll say."

"She's a nice girl, Colin," I say, wanting to make that perfectly clear.

"Yeah, so don't go fucking hurting her, okay?" he says.

I laugh, but I like that he's protective of her. "You're one to talk."

"Hey," he says. "The ladies know what they're getting into when we go out, Jesse."

He's right, they do, and I give him credit for that. A little girl comes running over with her mom, and one of the firefighters gives her a boost into the cab of the truck. My heart squeezes at the delight on the child's face. Kylie had been hoping for a little girl. Me? I was good either way as long as the baby was healthy, and I love my son more than life. I'd like to give him a sibling, but don't see that happening any time soon or ever. I bite back a humorless laugh. I don't even have a woman in my life, and dating or finding one is not on my agenda, making future kids out of the question.

"So you don't want to settle down, have a family?" I ask Colin.

He gives a noncommittal shrug, shades the sun from his eyes and glances around as cars fill the parking lot. "If I meet the right girl, sure."

Could Olivia be that girl?

I want that for her, and if she can have it with Colin, a guy she's totally into, then great. So why then, is my fucking stomach twisted into knots. It makes no sense.

I check my watch. "It's getting busy. I'd better let you get at it, and get my ass inside to help with the pancakes."

"You coming to the game tonight?"

"Probably not," I have to say, I do miss playing cards with the guys on Saturday night, but my grandmother is not getting any younger and she does enough for Lucas and me as it is. "I don't have a sitter." It's not like I can leave my son with just anyone. Any kind of disruption is hard on him.

"Why don't you ask Olivia to watch Lucas?"

"I'm not about to—" I shut my mouth when the sound of Olivia's voice stops me.

"Not about to do what?"

She sets a stack of pancakes, syrup and paper plates beside the pitchers of water, and Colin forks a couple onto one of the plates.

"Jesse never gets out to play cards anymore," Colin says. He winks at Olivia. "I miss taking all his dough."

"Asshole," I say and give him a shove. He laughs as he takes a big bite of his pancake, but it turns to a moan after he swallows.

"These are delicious," he mumbles, cutting into the fluffy pancake.

Olivia smiles up at him. "Thanks."

His head lifts and the corners of his mouth turn up as he looks at Olivia. "I never knew you were such a good cook."

"They're just pancakes, Colin." She gives him a hard eye roll and turns to me. "What aren't you about to do?"

"Colin suggested I ask you to babysit Lucas tonight so I can play cards with the guys, but I'm not—"

"Sure, I'll do it."

"You don't have to."

"I don't mind at all. It's the least I could do for you considering..."

"Considering what?" Colin asks, nosey bastard that he is.

"Nothing," I say quickly and pull her to me. I press my lips to hers and her hands automatically go around my back. Since I don't like to do anything half-assed, I kiss her. Hard. Like a man possessed. Yeah, if she wants me to play the part of adoring boyfriend to wake Colin the fuck up, I damn well plan to do a good job of it.

"Whoa, get a room already," Colin says, laughing.

I break the kiss and Olivia's cheeks are pink. "What was that for?" she asks quietly as a group of women come over and Colin walks away with them. Man, that guy is like a match to dry tinder, setting fire to all the women around him.

"For show," I tell her.

"Oh, well. I didn't know we had to kiss again so soon."

"You want Colin to stand up and take notice, right?"

"Well, yeah." She tugs her bottom lip between her teeth.

"Then this is what we have to do."

Yeah, kissing her just now had everything to do with Colin and our fake relationship. It had nothing to do with those lush lips of hers and how they've been occupying my thoughts since I first tasted them.

Whatever you need to tell yourself, dude.

"Okay, um, so yeah. I'd be happy to watch Lucas tonight." She pokes my chest. "You should go out with the guys. You don't have any fun anymore."

Kissing her was fun.

But I keep that thought to myself.

"If you're sure," I say. I hate to ask too much of anyone. Lucas is my responsibility, not hers, but I haven't left the house in so damn long. A night with the guys will help clear my thoughts. I'm sure of it.

"Of course."

"Come for dinner, then. We'll settle Lucas in together." She smiles like she likes that idea, but her eyes narrow and her hand goes to her stomach. "You okay?"

She shakes it off. "Yeah, fine."

"Tell Jack we're having lasagna."

"You want me to bring Dad?"

"Of course.

Warmth and appreciation move over her face. "That's thoughtful, Jesse."

"You can't leave him alone. Last time you left him to fend for himself, he nearly burnt down the kitchen." I lean into her and when I catch her sweet scent, I wish I hadn't. I took her clothes out of the dryer this morning, and they were infused with her aroma. "Unless that's part of your plan. Let your dad set the kitchen on fire to get the fire department to come over."

She laughs. "No, that's not the plan at all, and we already have one in motion. Dad will be happy to come for lasagna." She crinkles her nose. "About Dad."

My heart jumps. "Is he okay?"

"Oh yeah," she says quickly. "Nothing like that. I just... how do we handle this." She waves her hand back and forth between the two of us. "Word travels fast at the pub, and I don't want him to get the wrong idea. You know he's always trying to set me up."

"He just wants you to find someone who makes you happy."

She pauses as one of the firefighters sounds his alarm in demonstration.

"I know, but…"

"Maybe we just let him believe it," I suggest. "That way he'll get off your back about dating and marriage."

"I guess it would be nice to have the summer off from him badgering me." She shakes her head. "You know, I saw him on a dating site. I thought it was for him. Heck, I'd be happy if he was dating, but *noooo*, he was trying to set up a profile for me. Can you imagine?"

I laugh, even though it's not funny. "No, I can't." I don't blame her for being pissed off. I wouldn't want anyone meddling in my private life either. "It's settled then. We'll let him believe it."

She's about to leave, but turns back and says, "I have to get another key made after work. Mine is nowhere to be found. Need me to pick anything up?"

"Nope. It's all good. I've got everything under control."

She turns to leave, and my gaze drops to her sweet, curvy ass. A groan I have no control over climbs out of my throat, and I'm glad the chorus of kids all clamoring for a ride on the truck drown it out.

For the first time in a long time, I'm not sure I do have everything under control. As Olivia sashays away, she bends to pick up a runaway napkin. My damn pants tighten. Yeah, no, I don't have everything under control. I glance down and give a big thanks to my dick for driving that point home.

5

OLIVIA

From across the table, Dad rubs his belly. "I have to hand it to you, Jesse, you do make a great lasagna."

"Mom's old recipe," Jesse says as he sets his fork down. "Handed down from generation to generation." He gives Dad a teasing wink. "I could tell you what I put in it but then I'd have to kill you."

"Liar," I say and laugh as Lucas momentarily stills beside me at the table, his last bite of pasta inches from his mouth. He stares straight ahead, looking at nothing in particular as he tries to process his father's words. He's such a sweet boy who takes everything so literally. It has to be painfully hard to live in a world where expressions he doesn't quite understand are a huge part of our language. But Lucas is intelligent, and Jesse is doing his best to educate those around him. He's quick to stop misconceptions head on so people don't put his child into a box. Even without a mother, Lucas will grow up to live an independent life, I'm certain of that. Still, every boy needs a mother, so does every girl, and I know firsthand what it's like going through life without one. I was fortunate enough to have Jesse's mom take me under her wing.

"Kidding, Lucas," Jesse says not missing a beat. Even in conversation, Jesse is so aware of his son's thoughts and movements. With a frown still wrinkling his forehead, Lucas tugs on the neck of his T-shirt, a familiar habit, and slides his fork into his mouth.

I continue with, "Angela made this, didn't she?" Angela is the head cook at the pub. She's a sweetie, and a couple years older than me—she was classmates with Jesse—and getting married in less than a month. I checked 'no' for my plus one, but if Jesse and I are still pretending by then, perhaps we'll go together. OMG, wait! I haven't really thought this pretend relationship through. If Colin *does* stand up and take notice of me, what does that mean...

Jesse grins, pokes his thumb into his chest, and says, "Hey, I've got skills."

All thoughts of Colin evaporate and my lips tingle as soon as those words leave Jesse's mouth. I resist the urge to swipe my tongue over my bottom lips to see if his warm, intoxicating taste still lingers. Yeah, the man definitely has skills, and I have no doubt he's good at numerous other things. A fine shiver moves through my body as I imagine his talents—in the bedroom. I'm not a virgin, although I might as well be. The guy I fumbled around with in college left me with bad memories, and the need to finish solo—and at the time I wasn't even great at that. Neither one of us knew what we were doing, and it's an experience I never want to recreate.

Jesse, however... I bet he'd know his way around his woman's body without a navigation system guiding him, or the use of overhead illumination. Like I want all my jiggling parts on display. Yeah, when that college boy suggested we turn the lights on so he could see what he was doing, I quickly shut him down. Jesse however, those deft hands could undoubtedly find...

Stop thinking about him like that.

We might have been friends since we were kids, but he's my best friend's ex. Just thinking about his skill between the sheets goes against girl code. Yeah, I get that she left him, but still, these thoughts and fantasies are wrong.

Then why did his kisses feel so right?

"Yeah, Angela made it," I say, a statement not a question. When Jesse hired her last year, she revived the menu and added touches of her Italian heritage.

"I plead the fifth," Jesse teases and lifts his chin an inch.

"Can I have ice cream?" Lucas asks, and sets down his glass of water.

"Ice cream sounds great," I say, and jump up. Needing a distraction, and to cleanse my wayward thoughts, I go to the freezer and pull out a tub. I do love that the man keeps a freezer full of ice cream. "Chocolate chip okay?" I ask and Lucas gives me an enthusiastic nod. "Dad, would you like a scoop?"

My father rubs his belly again. "Like you even have to ask."

I laugh. "Right. What was I thinking?"

Earlier today, I let Dad know Jesse and I were sort of seeing each other. He acted surprised, but the Oscar still goes to Jesse and his performance in the parking lot. Maybe Tara told Dad already. I sensed that he knew...something. Yeah, Tara probably spilled the beans. She's not great at keeping things to herself and probably told Dad to act surprised. As long as she stays hushed on the fact that we're pretending, we'll be A-okay.

I think...

"Lucas," Jesse says, as I scoop out dessert, "You remember Olivia is going to watch you tonight, right?"

"Right," he says. "I want to read T-Rex," he says, and holds his hands up and growls.

"We can do that," I say and put his bowl in front of him. "Is that your favorite?"

He nods, and my heart wobbles a bit. Every day he looks more and more like his dad. He's going to be a heartbreaker with those big blue eyes.

"We're going to see the dinosaur show," Lucas says, and digs into his ice cream.

"A dinosaur show," I say, injecting enthusiasm into my voice for Lucas' sake. Dinosaurs are so not my thing. "Wow, that sounds amazing."

"You're coming," Lucas says, his head still down, his sole focus on digging a chocolate chip from the ice cream, and I glance at Jesse.

I arch a brow, used to Lucas blurting things out like that. "Am I now?"

"Next weekend, there is a show at the museum." Jesse casually rolls one broad shoulder. "I'm sure it will be boring for..."

"We're having a picnic, too. In the park. Dad said so. He's going to make peanut butter sandwiches. They're my favorite."

I throw my hands out. "Well then, if peanut butter sandwiches are involved, how can I say no?"

"It's a no-brainer," Jesse says as he grins at me and my stupid heart flutters.

Careful, Olivia.

"You sure?" Jesse asks, his blue eyes narrowing, assessing me. God, when he looks at me like that. How's a girl not to go all squishy inside? Tara was right. This man is the hottest ticket in town—the most eligible bachelor who seems hell bent on keeping that status.

Can I blame him? Not really. He's right to be careful who he brings into his child's life, and not every woman wants—or has what it takes—to understand his special needs son. Sadly, it wasn't what his own mother signed on for. My throat tightens at that thought and I swallow against the rawness. Lucas deserved so much better. So did Jesse.

I stare at him like he's dense. "Ah, peanut butter," I say, and he laughs. He gives me a dubious look and I lower my voice. "I leave in two months, Jesse. I want to spend as much time with Lucas as possible." My stomach squeezes. The thoughts of moving away from Lucas...from Jesse...sort of leaves a hollow in my gut, but I was accepted to Stanford and Dad needs the warmer climate. Even if I didn't want to go, I have to for my father's health. But there will be nothing easy about saying goodbye to the house I grew up in, and to my neighbors. There is a part of me that feels like I'm abandoning them too, in much the same way Kylie did, and haven't they both had enough loss already.

I nod as Dad's spoon clatters in the bowl. "I can take care of these dishes if you two have other things to do."

Jesse checks the clock. "I should probably get going. You can leave the dishes. I'll do them when I get back."

I nod. If I protest, he'll protest. I wave him off. "Go. Have fun."

"I shouldn't be too late."

"Stop worrying. Lucas and I will be fine." The man asks so little of me, it's the least I can do. Besides, I have no social life, so what's the difference in hanging out here or hanging with Dad at home. He's not even going to be there anyway, and Jesse has better stations than we do.

"I know he will be." I smile. The compliment means a lot. He turns his attention to his son as he starts making growling noises. "Lucas, go brush your teeth, get into your pajamas, and hop into bed. Olivia will come read your favorite book soon."

Lucas slides from his chair, and seconds before he darts from the room, Jesse says, "Are you forgetting something?"

Lucas groans and walks into his father's open arms. Looking so small in his dad's embrace, Lucas just stands there and stares at the ceiling as Jesse hugs him and drops a kiss onto the top of his mussed-up hair. Lucas abhors haircuts—as most kids do—and that's putting it mildly. Jesse breaks the hold and Lucas makes a beeline for the stairs.

"He's such a good kid," I say, and my stomach squeezes, a reminder that I'll never have children of my own. "You're doing such a great job with him, Jesse."

"Yeah," Jesse says quietly, a strange look on his face. Is he thinking about the difficulties in being a single father, or how Kylie went to Hollywood to make it big? While I've yet to see her in anything, Hollywood is cutthroat and I do worry about her well-being.

I ran into her parents a few months ago. They haven't even heard from her—or so they say. It's possible they're lying. They soured on Jesse when he gave everything up to run the bar, and the last time Jesse brought Lucas to visit them, Lucas had a colossal meltdown. I don't think Kylie's parents are bad people, they just have no idea how to interact with their grandson, and that day, with the dog barking and them insisting he go swimming, refusing to take no for an answer, Lucas became overstimulated and it triggered an emotional reaction.

I stand to clear the dishes, and we both reach for the same water glass. Jesse's fingers brush mine. I take a fast intake of breath and hope it goes unnoticed, but suspect Dad heard it when he climbs from his chair and makes a clicking sound with his tongue.

"I guess I should leave you two lovebirds alone," he says, his hoarse laugh echoing around us.

"Lovebirds?" I say. "Really, Dad?"

"Looks to me like Jesse wants to give you a kiss good-night, but isn't sure about doing it in front of your old man."

Dad steps up to Jesse and puts a gnarled arthritic hand on his shoulder. "It's about time you two got together, I'd say."

A niggling of guilt works its way through my stomach. I don't necessarily think Dad's been holding out for Jesse and me to get together. More like he just wants me to find *someone*. He's old-fashioned like that, but I don't need a man to be happy or complete. I'm an independent woman who knows the only one responsible for my happiness is me, and maybe this pretend relationship is a bad idea.

Maybe?

Yeah, it's definitely a bad idea.

Don't you just love them?

Honestly, I wouldn't know. I'm a bookworm. A nerd. A girl who never crosses the street when the 'don't walk' sign flashes, always returns her library books on time, and files her taxes long before the deadline.

Time to change that, Olivia.

Well, except for the library books. I mean come on...books.

Dad shuffles into the other room. "Heidi is picking me up here for bingo. I'll just flick on the TV and give you two some privacy."

When Dad rounds the corner—all the while whistling a tune, and I haven't heard him whistle in years—Jesse's head dips and his blue eyes move over my face. "You okay?"

"Maybe this isn't a good idea. I don't want Dad getting his hopes up about us. He seemed rather happy that we were together. He's whistling, for God's sake."

Jesse nods. "I get it. I don't want that either. Do you think we should stop?"

Say yes, Olivia.

Say yes right now.

But ooh, those kisses...

Before I can open my mouth—and likely say no—Jesse

dips his head. His warm lips find mine for a soft, exploratory kiss that weakens my knees. My nipples swell, press against his cotton T-shirt, a telltale sign of what he does to me. Can he feel my arousal?

Lucas growls from upstairs, mimicking his beloved T-Rex and I back up an inch. "What are you...doing?" I ask, working to hide my breathlessness, and what this man does to me.

He runs his hands through his hair, like he too is flustered. He shakes his head as if to clear it, and I'm impressed at how quickly he's able to pull himself together. Me? I'll be rattled until Sunday morning, a week from tomorrow.

He gestures with a nod. "Your Dad. He was watching. You hesitated when I asked if you thought I should stop, so I took that as a no. He was kind of waiting for me to make my move."

"Make your move?" A tight laugh climbs from my throat.

"I've got moves," he says, showcasing that cute dimple.

I swallow. Hard. "I guess we've come this far then, right?"

"Yeah," he says, that one hoarse word sliding over my flesh to take up residence between my quivering legs. Looks like Mr. Right will be coming out of my nightstand tonight. The toy does the trick, and while I have no desire to fumble around in the dark with anyone, the feel of a man's hands on my body, or even just holding me would be nice once in a while.

Dad flicks through the stations until he comes to the sport station, and he cheers when he catches the highlight reel on a soccer game.

Jesse backs up an inch. "I'd better head out."

"Bring lots of money."

He frowns at me. "Why?"

"Colin did say he missed taking your dough."

He grins. "He's a lucky bastard," he says with a grin, but a second later his eyes cast downward and his smile dissolves.

Whoa, what was that all about? "Okay, I'm out of here." He snatches his keys from the hook by the kitchen door and heads outside. My focus remains on his tight backside as he goes, and a sigh I have no control over catches in my throat as the setting sun falls over him. He backs out of the driveway, and Heidi pulls in behind him.

"Dad, Heidi is here," I call out, and the old leather recliner in the living room clicks as he lowers the lever and stands.

I step into the other room as he heads for the front door. "Jackpot is a big one tonight," he says and rubs his hands together. "Sure would go a long way in helping with Stanford."

My heart hitches. He's such a good man. He's been there for me my whole life, playing the role of mother and father. He definitely knows what Jesse is going through. Dammit, I hate lying to him. Hate it with the power of a thousand burning suns.

"Listen, Dad, about Jesse and me—"

He holds his hands up to cut me off. "Your love life is none of my business."

I snort out a laugh. "Oh, yeah. Since when?" He gives me a sheepish look. "Did you forget I caught you setting me up a dating profile?"

He waves twisted fingers at me. "You took that all wrong. I was just playing, trying out the site. Couldn't remember my birthday so I used yours."

"And my picture?" I roll my eyes. I'm not going to argue with him. I'd never win anyway. "Whatever you say." He goes serious, so serious my heart slows to a crawl. "What?" I ask.

He puts a warm palm on my cheek. "You and Jesse. I support you in whatever you do. You know that, right?"

"I know."

I love you, kiddo."

Hot tears prick my eyes. "I know that too, and I know

you want what's best for me," I say. I want what is best for
him to, which is one of the reasons I chose Stanford. It's
my dream school for sure, but if it was somewhere cold, a
place that would be detrimental to Dad's health, I wouldn't
go.

"You're a smart girl. You make good choices. You'll know
what to do when the time comes."

Unease worms its way through my veins. "Uh..." I'm about
to ask him what he means, when someone raps on the door.

"That's my ride. Wish me luck."

"Good luck," I say, and give him a kiss on the cheek.

He walks to the front door and I stand there staring after
him. What the heck was he talking about, and why is he
being so cryptic?

Footsteps pound from upstairs, and I hurry to the
kitchen, load the dishwasher and head upstairs to meet Lucas
in his room.

"Hey Lucas," I say. "Did you pick out a book?"

He holds it up and pats the mattress. The gesture makes
me smile. He's so much like his father. I settle in next to him,
and for the next half hour we read. The whole time he twists
a long strand of my hair between his fingers, like he always
does when we're seated close. He lets loose a big yawn and I
close the book.

"Time for sleep." When I was young and used to babysit,
I'd always say, don't let the bed bugs bite, but not in Lucas'
case. It would most certainly freak him out.

"Night, Lucas."

I walk to the door, and I'm about to close it.

"Olivia?"

"Yeah."

"What does retarded mean?"

Worry washes through me and I step back up to his bed.
"Why do you ask?"

He tugs on the front of his pajamas. "Madelyn called me retarded. What does it mean?"

Oh God, how do I answer this and explain it correctly?

"First of all, you did the right thing by telling me." He nods. "You're a very smart boy, and sometimes other kids can do and say hurtful things to those who aren't like them. But you've done nothing wrong." Sweat breaks out on my forehead. I'm so not very good at this and I don't want to give the wrong advice. "How does it make you feel when she calls you that?"

"Angry."

"You're allowed to feel angry, Lucas," I say, moving his hair from his forehead. He doesn't usually like being touched by me, he allows it this time.

He scrunches up his face. "I want to hit her."

"I understand that. What she is doing is hurtful, but hitting is not going to help. I'm really proud of you for not hitting, Lucas." I pause and then ask, "Is Madelyn in your day camp?" In the summers, Jesse puts Lucas in three afternoons a week. Lucas normally doesn't like to go, but he needs the interaction.

"Yes."

"I think your Dad should talk to your camp counselor. Would you be okay with me telling your Dad about Madelyn?"

He nods. "Caleb says I should ignore her."

I smile. "Caleb is a good friend, and he cares about you. Sometimes ignoring it doesn't make the problem go away, though. Sometimes we can't always solve the problem ourselves either. If she says it again, just know it's not anything you've said or done."

He yawns. "Okay."

"You stick with Caleb at day camp, okay?"

"We like to swing on the bars. Caleb thinks he's a

monkey," he says and laughs. I smile at that and hand him his stuffed dinosaur. He takes it into his arms and squeezes.

"Good night, Lucas."

"We're going to have peanut butter sandwiches when we go see the dinosaurs."

"I know. I can't wait."

"Me too."

I tuck him in again, and step into the hall, leaving his door cracked the way he likes it. I head down the hall, my heart painfully tight. I understand bullying, to a certain degree. When I was in seventh grade, one of the mean girls started picking on me. Later that week, Jesse sat at my table and had lunch with me. The teasing stopped, and to this day, I'm pretty sure Jesse making an appearance had everything to do with it. I'm also pretty sure he'd done it on purpose. Even when he was young, he was always aware of the things going on around him.

I stop outside his bedroom, and glance over my shoulder. My goodness, I feel like a child about to get caught with their hand in the cookie jar. A yawn pulls at me. I'm sure he wouldn't mind me taking a fast nap in his bed. Heck, I'll probably be up and in front of the TV when he gets home and he'd be none the wiser anyway.

Or not...

6

JESSE

The house is quiet when I enter, the dishes cleaned from the table. I'm not at all surprised by that. I call out to Olivia and wait for a reply. When no response comes, I step into the living room to find the TV off, but the lights still on, like someone left in a hurry. My thoughts instantly go to Lucas, and I fight off a burst of panic. Olivia is responsible. One of the most responsible people I know. If anything happened to Lucas, she'd have called me. Chances are she fell asleep while reading to him. I know I've dozed off a time or two.

I take my shoes off and quietly take the stairs two at a time, I'm about to walk past my bedroom when a bundle on my bed catches my eye. I turn and spot Olivia curled up in my bed, looking warm, lush and so inviting, and a hot wave of need grips me.

Fuck me.

I swallow against a tight throat, and force my legs into motion. I move down the hall to check on Lucas. When I find him fast asleep, I go back to my bedroom. I quietly cross the room and stand over sleeping beauty, taking my time to admire her.

Do I wake her?

She's been working so hard, I'm not sure I have the heart to rouse her from her slumber and send her home. Maybe I'll let her sleep here, and I'll go pass out on the sofa. I stand there a moment longer, my gaze tracking over her T-shirt and yoga pants. My God, the girl has curves I'd like to sink my fingers and teeth into. Talk about an insta-boner—a traitorous boner that is encouraging me to go for it.

But that would be so fucking wrong.

She's not accustomed to occasional hookups. That thought almost makes me laugh. Yeah, I'm not accustomed to them either, not anymore anyway.

She makes a sound in her sleep, a moan of sorts and flips over restlessly. Her eyelids flutter, her chest rising and falling rapidly. Jesus, is she having a nightmare? She whimpers again, her fingers digging into my bedding.

I lower myself and perch on the side of the mattress, not wanting to startle her. She flips over and faces me, her eyes pinched tight, and this time I'm pretty sure she's having some kind of night terror. I lightly touch her arm, find her skin hot to the touch.

"Olivia," I whisper, and she stills. "Olivia, I think you're having a bad dream."

With her chest rising and falling rapidly—and yes, I'm doing my damndest not to stare at her lush breasts, and failing miserably thank you very much—she opens one eye and then the another.

"Jesse," she murmurs. Catching me off guard, she inches up, and puts her hands around my neck. Her hot fingers tug on my hair as she drags me to her, her lush lips inches from mine as she falls back onto the pillow. Her breath rushes over my skin, stirs my aching cock. "Please..." she murmurs.

What the hell?

Fuck, maybe she's not having a nightmare at all. Maybe she's having a sex dream, and those are moans of want, not moans of fear. She squirms, and I shift until I'm on top of her, pressing her into the soft mattress with my hardness. And right now, I have a whole fucking lot of hardness—all centered between my legs.

Her tongue slips inside my mouth, tangles with mine, and my world spins on its axis. My God, she's warm and needy and I could kiss her sweet mouth for an eternity.

"Jesse," she whimpers again as her long legs slide around my ass. Need zaps my balls as she lifts her hips, and presses her hot core against my raging cock. Christ. I should put a stop to this. I need to put a stop to this.

Then why the hell aren't I?

I push her hair from her face, note her closed eyes and the needy moans spilling from her throat. Could this woman be any hotter? For a girl who is a bookworm, a brilliant student, it surprises me how goddamn oblivious she is to her sexuality. Truthfully, she's sexy on a whole other level. I briefly pinch my eyes shut. I somehow knew underneath it all, when this woman let go of her inhibitions, she'd be wild, and free, so damn open in the bedroom, it would fuck a man over in more ways than one.

The gentleman in me urges me to stop this, my cock however...

Wake her up, dude?

"Olivia," I whisper, and her moans fade away. She blinks, and I can tell the instant awareness seeps in by the way her body stiffens. "I think you were dreaming," I say, and my cock screams at me from between my legs, telling me to stop being a pussy-ass gentleman and give this woman what she wants.

But this is Olivia.

Heat and electricity arcs between us, and while I should

pull away, I can't seem to bring myself to do it. And why is that? Oh, because I want to fuck her in the worst way.

"Yeah," she murmurs.

"What were you dreaming about?"

Light shines in through my open curtains, highlighting the flush on her cheeks. Oh, yeah, she was definitely having a sex dream. Wait. My muscles go tight. Was she dreaming of Colin? Why the fuck does that thought bother me so much?

She called your name, dude.

She blinks rapidly. "I...nothing. I don't remember."

I should let this go, but I can't. I don't know why, or maybe I do. "I think you were having a sex dream."

I run my tongue over my lips, to taste her sweetness again. She groans and puts her hands over her face.

"Hey," I say as I gently tug them away and when I pin them to her sides, a fine shiver goes through her, telling me so goddamn much about her wants and needs. My heart pumps a whole lot faster, crashes against my ribs as I visualize the way I want to hold her down hard and do dirty things to her.

"You can tell me," I say softly. "We go way back. No judgement. I promise."

She tugs on her bottom lip with her teeth. "Okay, I...it's just...I was probably dreaming because I haven't been with anyone for a very long time," she admits.

I nod and not wanting her to feel alone in this, I say, "I know the feeling."

"I know you do." She swallows and averts her gaze. "I actually haven't been with anyone since college." She's not telling me anything I already don't know—Kylie wasn't great at keeping her best friend's secrets—but *why* is she telling me this? I'm not sure, but one thing I do know is when I pinned her hands to the bed, it brought hunger to her eyes. Not to mention last night, when I held her legs down on the sofa. That same raw need spread across her gorgeous face. Damned if I don't want to be the guy to take her where she needs to go and satisfy all those unanswered desires.

She snorts. "That experience was pretty horrible, actually."

I study her face and get the sense there is more going on with her, something she's hiding from me. Deciding to get to the bottom of the matter, I ask, "Do you think that's the only reason you were dreaming about sex? Because it's been a while?"

Her gaze moves over my face and I don't miss the unease in her dark eyes. Worry lingers there, and she shifts uneasily beneath me. "About Colin—"

"Oh, shit I get it," I say as one working brain cell kicks into gear. "You're worried about hooking up with Colin."

"I don't want—"

"To come off as inexperienced." I nod. "I get it."

Her mouth opens and closes as she stares up at me with those big doe eyes of hers. I shift and my raging hard-on presses against her leg. Her eyes go wide, now fully aware that if she's game to take this further, I'm game too.

"Jesse?"

"Yeah?"

"You're...*hard.*"

"No shit," I say and we both laugh a little nervously. "I come home and find you here in my bed, all warm and sexy and moaning. How can I not be hard?"

"Right, it's been a while," she murmurs, a line in her forehead as she frowns.

"Seriously? You think I'm hard because it's been a while?" I shake my head. "You really don't know how sexy you are, do you?"

Long lashes fall and open rapidly, like she's trying to wrap her brain around that. Yeah, I get it. I've never come straight out and said she was sexy before. It sort of goes against keeping things in the friend zone and all, but right now, with my dick outing me, revealing one very big secret, I think we've moved beyond that. I just can't let this ruin anything between us. As I think about that, a ridiculous, stupid, idiotic plan forms in my pea brain.

It's the worst plan in the world and if I knew what was good for me, I'd shut it down now.

"I can help you out," I say.

Dude, what the fuck are you doing?

"Help me out?"

I casually roll my shoulder and work to keep my voice steady while a storm rages inside me. "Well, we're both kind of here in my bed, both you know..."

"Aroused?"

"Yeah, and neither one of us has been with anyone in a while. We can sort of kill two birds with one stone."

One very big, *hard* stone.

"Two birds?"

"I can put my cock in you, Olivia. Give us what we both obviously need, and while I'm doing it, I can give you the experiences you want—the lessons. You know, so when you and Colin finally hook up, you'll be sure of yourself, confident, know what you like and dislike, know how you want to please your guy."

"I...uh..."

I study her face, the sexy flush on her cheeks. "That's what you want, right?"

I'm honestly not sure whether I want her to say yes or no. We're crossing a line here, and I'm man enough to admit it's motherfucking frightening.

She wets her mouth, her gaze dropping to mine, like she's dying to kiss me again. "It's a bad plan, Jesse," she says, but dammit, her eyes and the subtle movements in her body tell a completely different story. She wants this as much as I do.

"I know." I brush my thumb over her kiss swollen lips. "Then I guess we're doing it, huh?"

Fuck, I need her to say no as much as I need her to say yes.

A beat of silence as need and heat buzzes between us.

"Yeah, we're definitely doing it."

My cock jumps and my insides feel like they're being tossed around inside a dryer drum.

Is this really happening?

"One thing. We don't let this come between our friendship." I move a strand of hair from her face. We have to be on the same page here, because if she doesn't agree, I'm going to call abort. I want her, but no goddamn way am I going to risk ruining what we have between us. "We protect our friendship at all costs, okay?"

She nods. "I want that too. We can never let anything come between us, Jesse."

"One more thing."

"Yeah?"

"I want you to moan for me. I want you to let me know what you like, and how you like it. I don't want you to be shy or hold back, okay?" I touch her neck, and her skin sizzles beneath my hand.

"Okay," she murmurs, but I sense her trepidation.

"Olivia?"

"Yeah?"

"Can I put my cock in you now?" Her body heats beneath me, and I trail my finger down her arm, across her stomach, and toy with the band on her yoga pants. "After I've kissed every inch of you, of course." Yeah, I plan to fuck that trepidation right out of her until she's a quivering mess beneath me, begging for what she wants.

Before she can answer, I take her arms and put them above her head. A little whimper catches in her throat as her fingers tighten around the slats in the headboard. "Keep them there."

"Jesse," she whimpers, the urgency in her voice telling me all I need to know.

Deciding to play with her, I say, "If you move them before I say you can, I might just tie them to the bedpost."

"Ohmigod," she whimpers, and I bite back a chuckle.

"Maybe I'll do that anyway." It's obvious she likes the idea. "Tie you up and have you at my mercy."

"Jesse..."

"Yeah?"

"I...I've never done that."

I angle my head, press an open mouth kiss to her collarbone. She quakes beneath me. "Are you saying you don't want to?"

A pause and then, "No."

Jesus, she's killing me here. With a new kind of urgency pressing in on me, I stand, tear open my pants, and kick them to the floor. Her gaze slides down my body, and her eyes go big when she's sees my raging erection behind my tightly stretched boxers. I reach behind my head and tug off my T-shirt.

She goes up on her elbows for a better view, and I move, step into the light slanting in through my open curtains. She's seen me shirtless before, but I've never seen her look at me the way she's looking right now, and I kind of like it. Maybe a little too much.

"Are you checking me out, Olivia?"

She averts her gaze. "Sorry."

I laugh. "Don't be sorry. The truth is, I like it."

Her gaze slowly moves back to my near nakedness. "You do?"

"Yeah, and I like looking too." I stand for a moment, and consider the path my hands and tongue will take on her body as I let her look her fill. "I can't see much in the dark, though."

"Leave the lights off," she says, a hint of panic in her voice.

"Yeah?"

She nods, her eyes dropping, and narrowing like she's struggling to see my erection. I peel my boxers off and take my cock into my hand. Her sweet little gasp makes me chuckle. Jesus, we're going to have so much fun. I stroke myself, and she whimpers and shifts, her body so achingly hungry—calling out to me in ways that are fucking with my mind and dick. Christ, I'm damn near ready to explode from the sight of her squirming as she watches me work my hand over my cock. But I don't want to rush this. No, I need to take it slow with her, give her the experience she's looking for.

"Can I..." she begins, but lets her words fall off.

"Can you what?" I ask. I give her a minute to respond, but she shies away. "No way. None of that. No holding back. We're friends. Ask whatever it is you want to ask. Be honest with me so I can make this good for you, and give you what you need."

"I...can I touch you?" she asks, and my dick jumps. Okay, that I wasn't expecting, and fuck yeah.

"You want to touch my cock?"

Her head bobs up and down, and even though she appears eager, I can sense her nervousness, feel the intimidation radiating off her in waves. Her innocence is a real mindfuck.

"You're sure you want to?" I ask.

"Yes," she says, her voice full of conviction.

I kneel on the bed, position myself between her legs. She sits up straighter, and her mouth is slightly parted as she takes me into her warm hands. I groan and toss my head back as she begins a slow exploration, weighing me, and testing my girth as she lightly rubs her fingers over my tightly stretched skin, taking her time to circle my crown, and outline every hard ridge.

"Fuck." I dip my head to see her. "That feels good, Liv," I say, as I visualize my cock between those lush lips. As if reading my thoughts, she leans forward and takes me into her mouth. I grip her mess of long curls, and follow the motion of her head as she takes me to the back of her throat. The heat of her mouth wraps around me, so goddamn good my dick jumps in her mouth. My cock aches, craving to be inside her hot pussy, but not wanting to put an end to this sweet torment. Fuck, I don't remember a blow job ever being so incredibly torturous before. She moans against my cock and the vibrations reach my aching balls. My heart crashes harder, and I take fast breaths as she takes me deeper, until I hit the back of her throat and she chokes. I ease my cock from her mouth.

"Easy," I say as my dick dangles inches from her gorgeous mouth. She crinkles her nose. "Hey, what's wrong?"

She dips her finger into my pre-come and spreads it over my crown. "I'm not very good at this, am I?"

"Are you fucking kidding me? I'm ready to shoot down your throat."

"Really?" she asks, her eyes widening.

"Yeah, really." I say and shake my head. "You are so goddam hot, Liv."

Before I can lay her out and have my way with her, she takes me back into her mouth. A moan catches in her throat as she sucks on me, a little more confidence in her as she explores me with her tongue. I let her lick me, cradle my balls, and take me as deep as possible. Yeah, I let her do all those things, all the while I'm silently reciting the alphabet so I don't lose control and shoot down her throat. I *need* to be inside her when I let go.

"Liv, you're going to have to stop. You're fucking killing me."

I pull back and my cock plops from her mouth. She wipes the dampness off her lips with the back of her hand, and even though that shouldn't be sexy, it is when she does it.

"My turn," I say and give her a little shove until she's on her back. "Yeah, my turn to touch you all over. You want that, don't you, Liv?"

"Yes," she says her voice needy and breathless.

"If I put my hand in your panties, am I going to find you all hot and wet for me?" She gulps. "Tell me."

"Yes," she says.

"Did sucking my cock turn you on?"

She puts her fingers to her mouth, like she can still feel my cock inside. "Oh, God, Jesse."

"Did it?" I push. She might be shy and innocent, but there's no doubt she likes it when I talk to her like this.

"Yes."

I settle myself beside her. "When I put my cock in here," I say, and slide my hand into her yoga pants, "you're not going to hold back, right? You're going to ride me hard, take what you need?" I toy with the band on her panties, pulling on them so they're snug against her clit.

"I am," she moans and her hips lift, so damn eager and responsive to everything I do.

I chuckle. "Good, so first things first." I reposition, and kneel between her legs. "These pants have to go."

"Yes, please," she says, her voice low and breathless, as her chest rises and falls erratically. Goddammit, I love how hot this woman is for me.

Me.

Not Colin.

But then one working brain cell reminds me this is to help her with Colin.

Shit, yeah right. I want her to find someone she can be happy with, but right now, in this moment with her writhing beneath me, her body mine to do with as I please, I don't want her to be thinking about anyone other than me, and all the pleasure I'm bringing her.

I slide my hands under her sweet ass, taking pleasure in her soft voluptuous shape as I tug her pants down, exposing her gorgeous curvy hips, and lacy underwear. Fuck, this woman is sexy. I want to jump up and turn the lights on to get a better look, but she wanted them off, and that would require me to get off the bed. Now that I've got her right where I want her, I'm not going anywhere. No, instead I'm going to savor every inch of her, until she's moaning my name and begging for more.

I toss her pants aside, and move deeper between her legs. I widen my fingers and dip beneath her T-shirt to slide it upward. She quivers when I reach her breasts, and I brush my thumb over her nipples. They swell and poke against her lace bra.

"Sit up?"

She immediately obliges, and I chuckle at the urgency in her, although who am I to talk? I suddenly feel like a hormonal teen about to get his rocks off for the first time. I can't decide if it's her innocence or eagerness that does that to me.

"Take your shirt off," I command in a soft voice.

She grips the hem and peels it over her head. I groan as she bares herself to me. I stare, my mouth watering as I gaze at her puckered nipples through her bra. She lifts her hands, like she's about to cover herself, uncomfortable under my careful scrutiny, but I shake my head no to stop her.

"Keep going," I say, and she reaches behind her back and unhooks her bra. I nearly bite my fucking tongue off as her full, lush breasts spill free. I just wish I could see them better. I guess I'll have to feel my way around.

"Beautiful," I say and give her a little shove until she's back on the pillow. Her hands creep up to grab the slats in the headboard, and a grin plays with the corners of my mouth. This sweet girl wants me to take charge.

Then take charge I will.

OLIVIA

I can't freaking believe this is happening. Tara was right. Sometimes bad ideas are the best. As I consider that, guilt niggles at me. Maybe I should have corrected him. It's obvious when I mentioned Colin's name, and was about to explain that I didn't really want to be with him, Jesse misunderstood. I should have come clean then and there, right?

His growl of want ripples over my breast, and that measure of guilt is quickly replaced by a new kind of excitement. Need races through my veins as he falls over me, his cock pressing hard against my leg as he swipes his hot tongue over one puckered nipple, and tweaks the other with his thumb and finger. I whimper and moan and lift my hips, so goddamn needy I fear I'm going to spontaneously combust.

How can I possibly rectify the situation now, when this is *soooo* good? When it comes right down to it, I am inexperienced, and would like to learn a little more in the bedroom.

Way to try and make this sound right, Olivia.

He flattens his tongue, and swirls it around my nipple and I feel the tug all the way to my core. I want this. I want him.

It might not be smart, and I fear there could be repercussions, but under the circumstances, my lust-rattled brain is beyond making any sort of rational decisions.

Yeah, this is for sure happening.

Forgetting everything—including girl code—I give in to the things this man makes me feel. Desperate to explore his body, my hands go to his hair and I rake my fingers through his soft strands, holding his mouth to my breast like some shameless woman out for all she can get. Is this out of character for me? I wouldn't know. I've only been with one guy, so I'm not really sure what I like, don't like, or how brazen or shy I'll act in the heat of the moment.

Speaking of heat...

He draws one nipple into his mouth, and lightly presses down with his teeth. Pain and pleasure mingle, and hit all my erogenous zones on a lazy path to my sex. He bites down a little harder, like he's testing me, and I moan. He slides his finger into my panties and circles my clit, teasing until I'm panting like a Saint Bernard in a hot car—in Hawaii.

"Please," I cry out, and arch up as he takes control of our play.

"Need something, Liv?" he asks, as my nipple pops from his hot mouth.

"You know I do," I say, and he parts my netherlips with deft fingers. This guy definitely knows his way around a woman's body. I jerk forward and his chuckle wraps around me.

"Hands on the headboard. Now."

I do as he commands, and he presses hot, open-mouth kisses to my stomach as one thick finger teases my sex with the promise of things to come. He toys with me, offering me his finger up to the first knuckle, but it's not enough, not nearly enough—especially after seeing what he's working with between his legs. I whimper and moan, ready to lose my ever-loving mind.

Touch me already.

"Something on your mind, Liv?" he asks as sexual frustration grips me hard. I lift my head and his deep sexy gaze bores into me, touching and awakening places that have been dormant my entire life. Never have I ever been so needy for anything—anyone.

"Put it all the way inside me, please," I manage to get out through my labored breathing.

"Ah, so that's what you want," he says and I never knew he was such a tease in the bedroom. Of course, I don't know anything about him in the bedroom—other than what I'd fantasized about over the years. But I guess that's all about to change.

"Yes."

"I can definitely help with that." He dips into me, and I let out a gasp as my eyes roll into the back of my head. He pushes deep, his thick finger widening me as the heel of his hand presses on my swollen clit. With Jesse, talented man that he is, there's no awkward fumbling, no banging of heads or uncomfortable silence in the dark. No, everything in the way he's touching me is perfection and all I'm experiencing is pure bliss.

I lift my hips, grind against his palm as I clench down on my teeth. Pleasure licks over my flesh, igniting every inch of my body. On fire for this man, I cry out. "That feels incredible."

"Yeah, it does," he says, and pulls his finger almost all the way out, only to slide it back in again. His low growl of pleasure nearly sends me over the edge. "You're so tight and wet, Liv. Do you have any idea what that does to me?"

His cock presses against my thigh, giving me a good indication, but do I dare tell him that being around him always makes me wet, always has? I fantasize about taking him into my mouth again, sucking on him until he comes down my throat. A hard tremor wracks my body. God, who knew that would turn me on so much. Honestly, there are so many things I want to try, to experience—with Jesse.

"You like this. You like getting fucked by my finger?" He moves his stiff finger in and out, long hard strokes that take me to the precipice so fast it leaves my head spinning.

"God, yes."

"Is there anything else you want in here?" he asks.

"I want your cock," I blurt out, and he grins.

"Good, because you're going to get it. Right after you come all over my hand and mouth so I can taste you."

As pleasure builds in my body—I clearly love this dirty side of Jesse—I can't believe how close I am to climaxing. I should probably be embarrassed, and I probably would be if I was rolling around with someone other than my neighbor. His complimentary words, and the way he touches me puts me at ease, makes me feel a little more comfortable in my own skin. He pulls his finger from my core, and I whimper at the loss.

"Jesse," I murmur, but my protest turns to a moan when he slides down the bed and puts his mouth on my sex. "I... holy God," I cry out. His masterful tongue glides over my clit as his finger once again finds its way inside me. He laps at me, licks me hard as he slides his finger in and out of my wetness. "Yes, like that. Just like that," I murmur, inhibitions a thing of the past.

He glances up at me, and I can just imagine how I look. Glazed eyes, flushed cheeks, my big breasts rising and falling with pleasure. It's dark in the room, so I'm not sure how well he can see, but I'm not interested in him turning on the lights, even though I'd love a better look at all his delicious nakedness.

He grins at me, like he's pleased with the state I'm in, like he's pleased he put this look on my face. He turns his attention back to my needy body, and a cry catches in my throat as he pushes another finger in for a deliciously snug fit. My moan of pleasure curls around us, and he growls, looking like *he*'s about to come undone from finger-fucking and tasting me.

"I'm so close," I cry out, my entire body quaking.

He applies more pressure to my clit, and brushes the rough pad of his finger over the hot bundle of nerves inside me, and a second later, my hips are off the bed, my clit banging against his face as I ride his finger. I gasp, the world closing in on me as my legs go weak, my hot juices spilling free, soaking his hand and face as he eases up on my clit, giving me space to ride out the pleasure.

"Yeah, that's it," he murmurs from deep between my legs. He licks at my sopping wet sex and breathes in the heady scent of my arousal as I lay there panting, reveling in each and every hard pulse between my legs, totally lost in the moment. My body finally stops spasming, and I go up on my elbows to glance at the man still between my legs. Heaven. That's the only way I can describe the sensations in my body.

"You were wrong. So fucking wrong," he says, and panic erupts inside me. What the hell was I wrong about? Agreeing to let him pretend to be my boyfriend, or falling into bed with him?

His head lifts, and his intense eyes lock on mine and steal my breath. "Yesterday you told me you weren't made of sugar, but you have to be otherwise you'd never be this sweet."

My God, who is this dirty talking, take-charge guy? He's so different from my gentlemanly neighbor, and I have to say I love this side of him just as much.

"I can't wait to get my cock in here." My pulse jumps as he moans, like he's savoring the taste of me. He swipes his tongue over his lip, and takes his cock into his hand again. My sex pulses in anticipation. I can't quite believe this is happening and that I'm finally going to feel this man inside me.

"Jesse," I gulp, and reach for him.

"You want this, Liv?" he asks, his voice so deep and hoarse, I barely recognize it.

He strokes his cock and I openly stare. "Yes, I want you inside me."

"You want me to fuck you?"

A violent quiver pulses through me as he trails his hand over my stomach, until he's touching my breasts. "These are so beautiful, I'd like to fuck them, but I need to be inside you right now." He toys with my full breasts, and squeezes one in his big hand. I blossomed early and the boys used to tease me relentlessly. I was always a little self-conscious of my size, but right now, with the way Jesse is staring at my breasts, like they're a prize to be treasured, it boosts my confidence.

"I've never done anything like that before," I say honestly.

He nods, like he already knows that, and leans over me to grab something out of his nightstand. "Your tits are perfect for fucking," he says, and I gulp air.

"Maybe that's something I'd like to try."

He tears into the little packet with his teeth and a second later he's rolling a condom onto his cock.

"Maybe?" he asks.

"If you're giving me lessons, Jesse. I think we should try everything, don't you?"

"Then you do want me to fuck these gorgeous tits?" He strokes my nipples.

"Yeah," I murmur.

He grips his cock harder, and his head goes back as he moves his hand up and down his shaft. Is he imagining his cock between my breasts, shooting off into my mouth? Heat rockets through me at the visual and I have to say, while I love the way he touched me, there is something so erotic in watching him touch himself. Is that strange? A weird fetish? God, I really am out of my element.

"Something on your mind?" he asks as he falls over me, holding me down with his weight. I lower my lashes. "Hey, don't be embarrassed. You can tell me anything." He cups my chin and lifts my face to his.

Serious eyes move over mine, a careful assessment. I trust Jesse, more than I've ever trusted anyone, and I want to be open and honest with him. "It's just...when you hold your cock like that, I kind of...I don't know. I think I like it."

That seems to please him. "Then let me tell you something. I'd love to watch you touch yourself, too. I'd love to stand here, watch you put your fingers into your sweet cunt, and rub your wet clit, but I'd come in seconds flat."

Holy God! "Really?"

"Yeah, really," he says with a shake of his head, like he can't believe that I'm questioning that. "You slay me, Liv. You're killing me with all these voluptuous curves, and all your sweet innocence."

"Jesse..."

"Yeah."

Bolder than I ever thought I could be I ask, "Can you put your cock in me now?"

"Jesus, woman," he says, and I can't help but chuckle. "You really are trying to kill me."

"No, I'm just trying to get you to fuck me."

"Baby, I'm going to fuck you so hard, you'll still feel me a week from now."

Excitement pulses through me and I put my hands on his shoulders to hang on. His muscles ripple as he widens my legs with his hips and positions his cock at my entrance.

"Ready for me?"

God, if he only knew for how long.

"Yes," I murmur and wiggle trying to force him in already. I used to have patience, up until about a minute ago. Yeah, I want this. I want him in ways that are frightening.

In one thrust, he buries himself inside me and I open my mouth, but no sound comes as he fills me to the hilt, gloriously stretching me like I've never been stretched before. He's right. I'm definitely going to be feeling him a week from now, and honest to God, I'm not sure if that's a good thing or not.

He inches out, and drives back in again, and I claw at him. He moans and moves his hips, long steady strokes that drive me wild.

"You are so hot and tight, I am not going to last," he growls into my ear, his hot breath burning over my flesh. I wrap my legs around him, our bodies entwined as his hands search for mine. He captures my wrists and flattens his palms over mine as he pushes my arms over my head. He lifts an inch, looks the length of my body, and pushes his cock in and out of me.

"Jesus, Liv. Watching my cock slide into you like this..." He stops to let out a breath. "It's fucking hot."

"I want to see."

He lets go of my hands and braces himself with one arm as I inch up. He powers forward, inching into me, and as I watch his gorgeous cock appear and disappear, my stomach clenches as pleasure sweeps through me. My God, is this what it's like to get fucked? Jesus, how will I ever go back to being celibate after tonight?

Who says you have to?

"So hot," I agree as his lips find mine again. He kisses me as I drop back onto the pillow, and my body heats up. He grins against me, his pelvis stimulating my clit, and my body convulses again, the second orgasm taking me by surprise. He breaks the kiss and growls into my ear.

"I feel you. You're coming all over my cock."

"So good," I murmur, and he drives into me with fast, hard blunt strokes that are for him now, as he chases his own orgasm. I move with him as he slides in and out of my slick sex. He inches back, almost all the way out, and I lift, needing him inside, needing the connection to the point that it's a bit scary.

He pumps some more, and then stills, high inside me. I close my eyes, concentrate on each pulse of his cock as he lets go. I nearly come again.

"So good, Jesse," I say and put my arms around him, hold his damp body to mine. He grunts and comes some more, and when he's depleted, he collapses on top of me and buries his mouth in the hollow of my neck. We stay like that for a long time, my heart racing.

He's way better in bed than I ever could have imagined. I hold him too and try not to overthink things as I ride out the bliss, but I can't help but wonder, was he only eager because it's been so long for him? I'm not sure, but I'm not going to spend time worrying about it. What we just did was fan-freaking-tastic, and judging by the way he came, he was as into it as I was, and I shouldn't care if it was only because he'd gone without for so long. I'm inexperienced and he's offering to be my teacher. Yeah, okay, so he thinks he's doing it to help me be a better lover for Colin, and while that's not entirely true, this will help me be a better lover for the next guy.

"I was thinking," I begin.

His head lifts, and his gorgeous eyes meet mine. "Yeah, about what?"

"About what you said about tying me up."

I open one eye and wince as the morning light shines in through my open window. Memories from last night bombard me and I turn, only to find the other side of the bed empty and cold to the touch. Did Olivia sneak out last night after we fell asleep? While there is a strange emptiness inside me at that thought, I realize it's probably for the best. Last night was a one-time thing, or at least I thought it was until she talked about tying her up. Maybe when her post-orgasm bliss wore off this morning, she had a change of heart.

I sit up and rub my eyes as I listen for sounds in the house, but all is quiet. Most times Lucas is up by now. But I don't hear his cartoons blaring, and he usually comes and gets me up for breakfast. I shove my covers off and pray to fucking God there is no awkwardness between us in the light of day. I know I went at her like a goddamn animal, and not just because I haven't been with anyone in a long time, but because seeing her naked fucked me over big time. Shit, if I ruined things...well, I don't know what I'd do without her in my life.

She's moving away soon, dude.

As that thought sours my stomach, I tug on a pair of sweats and grab a clean T-shirt from my dresser. I pad quietly to the door, and open it. Down the hall I can see that Lucas' door is wide open. A faint noise of dishes clanging reaches my ears. Is Lucas down there getting his cereal?

I head down the stairs and that's when I hear whispered voices, and my pulse jumps at the sound of Olivia's. In the kitchen, I find her emptying the dishwasher as Lucas eats his cereal at the table, a dinosaur book in front of him.

"Morning," I say, and Olivia turns my way.

"Did we wake you?" she asks. "We were trying to be quiet."

"Nope, woke up on my own." I cross the floor, ruffle my kid's hair and drop a kiss onto his forehead. He quickly wipes it away and I laugh. "Nice to see you, too."

"I've been learning all about velociraptors," Olivia says and my gaze goes to the light, scratchy beard burns on her face. Damn, I really kissed the hell out of her. I'm not sure how she's going to cover that up.

"You uh..." I reach out and smooth my hand over her sensitive skin. Did I leave my mark anywhere else on her body, perhaps someplace a little more intimate? "Does it hurt?"

"No." Heat crawls into her face. "I have some cream at home, and my foundation will cover it."

"Sorry about that," I say, and scrub my face.

"Don't be. I love your beard."

In need of coffee, I reach over Olivia's head to get a mug, and our bodies brush. Her little intake of air doesn't go unnoticed.

"I thought you'd left," I say.

"I was going to go home, but checked my bag and couldn't find a key. I must have a hole in my backpack, because I keep losing it. I just had a new one made last night, and put it in here before Dad and I came over and it's gone already."

I frown as I think about that. "Did you look around here? Maybe it fell out on the floor."

"I looked. It's nowhere."

I glance at my son, but don't think he'd go into Olivia's bag, and other than her father, no one had access to her things last night. "Strange."

She fiddles with the silverware as she places it in my drawer. "I need a new bag anyway. Mine is old and ratty and I probably should have thrown it out ages ago. I hope you don't mind that I'm still here. I didn't want to go knocking on the door and wake up Dad. He was probably out late at bingo. He likes to sleep in on Sunday."

I study her, and listen to her rattle on—something she does when she's nervous or uncomfortable. Another bout of worry invades me.

I pour a mug of coffee and refill her cup. "We okay, Liv?" I ask, wanting to hit the problem—if there is one—head on.

Her chest rises as her eyes lift to mine. "Yeah, we're okay," she says, a dreamy look on her face. "It's just...last night."

I brush up against her and my cock twitches. "It was pretty amazing."

"It was," she says, her voice low, breathless, like she's reliving the moments.

I pour milk into our cups and take a much-needed sip. "Nothing comes between us though, right."

"I wasn't sure how this morning was supposed to play out." She crinkles her nose, uncertainty spreading across her pretty face. She shrugs, and holds her hands up, palms out. "I didn't really know whether I should leave or stay, and then Lucas woke up, and I lost my key..."

I cup her elbow, and her quiver vibrates through me and zaps my balls. "I'm glad you're here, and nothing needs to be forced. Let's just let this play out the way it does. Do what we feel is best at the time. This is all to help you with Colin," I say, but maybe it's more of a reminder to myself.

"Yeah, Colin…" she says, but her voice drops off. Is there something she's trying to tell me? Maybe she's not sure where we go from here? Fuck, I'm not sure either.

"What happens next, it's your call. If you want this to be a one-time thing, we won't ever do that again." As soon as the words leave my mouth, my mind takes me on a journey, imagining her tied up while I fuck those lush breasts of hers. I cough to hide a groan. Olivia grins at me. Busted. "Okay, I'm not going to lie," I say my voice low, for her ears only. "I want more."

Dark lashes lift to reveal eyes full of desire. "I want more too," she says, but then her body stiffens. "I mean I have so much more to learn, right?"

"Right."

She arches a brow. "I never knew you were such a good teacher."

I step closer, inches from her body, and heat arcs between us. "It's easy when you have a great student."

Her face falls.

"Was it something I said?"

"No, I just…" She glances around me, to check on Lucas, but he's completely engrossed in his book. "Last night Lucas told me some girl in day camp was picking on him. She called him retarded. You might have to talk to the instructors or maybe the child's parents."

"Who was the girl?"

"Madelyn." I nod, and she asks, "Do you know her?"

"Yeah, I know her mother. They live a few blocks over. I met her when I was dropping Lucas off at camp. We talked a bit, and she actually wanted me to join her single parent group."

"Really?"

"Yeah, I told her I'd think about it, but I'm not interested. I'm already in a group that deals specifically with high-functioning autism. I'll talk to her first."

She jerks her thumb toward the back door. "I...uh, Dad should be up now. I should probably get going. I need to shower and change. I have the afternoon shift at the pub today."

I move closer, wanting to kiss the fuck out of her before she leaves, but can't with my son in the room. It would confuse him, and the world is hard enough on him as it is.

"I guess I'll see you there. My grandmother is watching Lucas this afternoon. I have some paperwork to go over."

She leans into me, all conspiratorial like. "You didn't happen to see my panties, did you? I couldn't find them this morning. I was fumbling around in the dark, and didn't want to turn the lights on and wake you."

"You mean to say you're not wearing panties?"

"No."

I stifle a groan. "I'll look for them. But if I find them, I just might keep them," I say.

She puts her hand on her hip, trying to look indignant, and not quite able to pull it off, not with that sexy, well-fucked look she's wearing.

She lifts her chin. "They're my favorites."

"Yeah, mine too," I say and chuckle.

She shakes her head, like she doesn't know me at all. But she does. Last night she just saw another side to me, and goddammit I want to show it to her again, sooner rather than later.

Easy, Jesse.

Fuck, I shouldn't want her this much. I'm helping her in the bedroom so she can perform for another guy, for Christ's sake. Whose stupid idea was that, anyway?

Oh, right. Mine.

Well, look at that. I'm a masochist *and* a dumbass.

"If you find them, I'd like them back."

"We'll see," I say.

She steps around me. "See you later, Lucas. Thanks for teaching me all about velociraptors."

"You're welcome."

She grabs her backpack and hikes it over her shoulder and gives me a smile before she leaves the house. I stare out the window after her and she must feel my gaze on her. She glances at me over her shoulder, and gives a little finger wave.

I take a breath to pull myself together, and drain the coffee in my cup before pouring another.

"Dad."

"Yes?" I ask.

"Why was Olivia here? She doesn't stay over when she babysits me."

Oh, my sweet observant boy. "I was late getting home and she fell asleep and so I just let her stay over." All true.

"She keeps losing her key."

"I know." I drop down into the chair next to him. "I have an idea. To thank her for watching you last night, maybe we can buy her a new bag."

He thinks about it for a moment. "She likes pink."

I laugh. "How do you know that?"

"She dumped her bag looking for her key, and she had a pink wallet and pink elastics for her hair."

Wow, my boy is far more observant than me.

"Okay, so you'll help me pick out a pink bag?"

He nods.

"All right. Go brush up and dress and we'll go to the mall. Don't forget your headphones," I say. The last time we went to the mall, he'd become overstimulated, and the counsellor in my parenting support group had suggested headphones. They actually helped with his sensory processing issues.

I finish another cup of coffee, and have a fast bowl of cereal. Over an hour later, with Lucas' bag packed with all his favorite things, and Olivia's new bag on the seat beside him, we head to my grandmother's place. Honestly, I don't know what I'd do without her.

Lucas flings his door open when I stop, and exits the car. Grandma steps out onto the porch to greet us. She gives Lucas a big smile, but he's not focused on her. He stomps up the steps, and before he steps inside, he blurts out, "Olivia stayed over last night."

Grandma's lips quirk as she casts a glance my way. "Well, well," she says. "It's about time you two finally got together."

I laugh to hide my uncomfortableness. "It's not like that." I pull Lucas' bag from the back and toss it over my shoulder. "She was babysitting and fell asleep." I head toward her and her eyes narrow. Jesus Christ, I'm sure she can see right through me and this is a conversation I'm not having with her.

I hand the bag over, and she clutches it. "If you want to have another sleepover with Olivia, I'd be happy to keep Lucas for the night."

I shake my head. "It's not like..." At seventy-five the woman is as astute as ever. No sense in arguing with her, either. "No, but thanks for the offer. He has day camp tomorrow afternoon, and I don't want to mess around with his routine."

She waves her hand at me. "Oh, honey. Sometimes a little messing around is what everyone needs."

My God, she did not just say that to me.

I give her a kiss on the cheek and she beams up at me. "You seem a little tired today. Didn't sleep well." She's grinning at me like the goddamn cat who ate the canary. I expect her to puff out a feather any second now.

"If anything happens, call, okay?"

"Of course, I will, but he'll be fine. I'm making his favorite for dinner tonight. You're the one I worry about."

"No need to worry about me. I'm all grown up, Grandma."

Yup, that's me. All grown up and suddenly making one bad decision after the other.

OLIVIA

Olivia

I tie my apron around my waist and spot Tara moving around the tables and coming my way. I need to play it cool. No, I *have* to play it cool. I don't want her knowing what Jesse and I did last night—and get the wrong idea, or the right idea, or any idea—even though I can't seem to stop thinking about it. How did I not know sex was so good? All the lost years, the lost orgasms. I chuckle at that thought and Tara arches a brow as she shimmies up next to me at the bar.

"Something funny?" she asks.

I give a fast shake to my head and my ponytail bobs around my shoulders. "Inside joke. You wouldn't get it."

She snaps her fingers and looks me over, a knowing grin on her pretty face. "No, but it looks to me like someone *got it*."

I swallow, and pray to god my eyes are not bugging out of my head, but I suspect they are. "What are you talking about?" My God, do I still have sex written all over me? I scrubbed my still tingling body clean this morning, lightly touching all the glorious bruised spots that continue to remind me of last night, and put on copious amounts of makeup to hide the burn on my face and neck.

"Your face. You have beard burns."

Crap.

I guess I didn't do a good enough job.

"Oh, no. It's not what you think it is," I fib, as pool balls clang in the adjoining room. The heavy front door opens and closed with a bang, and in walks Brit, another server. Brit, Kylie and I used to all be friends in high school, but we grew apart when Kylie and I went to college. Brit was always a little too dramatic for me, anyway. I wonder if she ever hears from Kylie. We don't really talk about her anymore, especially in front of Jesse.

Tara taps her fingers on the counter. "Then what is it?"

I point to my face. "Oh, this is just an allergy. New makeup. Sensitive skin." My God, what happened to honest Olivia? What kind of a human resource consultant am I going to be?

"Uh huh," she says, and leans into me like she's anxious to hear all the juicy gossip, but I'm not a girl who kisses and tells. "You guys hooked up way faster than I thought you would. Good for you, *gurl*."

I follow her gaze and spot Colin and a few of the other firefighters shooting a game of pool. Ah, she thinks Colin did this to me. An almost hysterical laugh bubbles in my throat. I should probably let her believe it, but rumors spread faster than brush fires in this place and Colin doesn't need to be in the middle of them when he's done nothing.

"No, we didn't hook up."

Her eyes go wide, then narrow in on me and I can almost hear the wheels spinning. "So are you saying the hottest bachelor in town did that to you?"

"I'm not saying anything of the sort," I say and she laughs, letting me know she's just playing with me.

"You are so easy to mess with," she says. "I'll trade sections with you tonight so you can go flirt with lover boy."

"Lover boy?" Brit asks, as she ties her hair back. "Who's lover boy? What's going on?"

"Oh, didn't you hear," Tara says. "Olivia and Jesse have hooked up."

Always the drama queen, her eyes go wide. "Are you kidding me?" She glances around until her eyes settle on Jesse who is chatting with customers at one of the tables. "Seriously, are you kidding me?"

"Why would we be kidding you?" Tara asks.

Brit shakes her head. "They're friends, and well..."

"Well what?" Tara asks, her teeth clenched.

"She just doesn't seem his type."

"Ah, I'm right here," I interject. "I can hear you both."

"You sound like you're jealous," Tara says, and Brit stiffens.

Good God, does she like Jesse? I'm not sure why that surprises me. Every woman is in love with the most unattainable, hottest bachelor in town.

"No, that's not it at all," Brit says, and gives a dramatic sigh as she walks away, tugging her phone from her apron as she goes.

I shake my head, once again feeling like that chubby girl that every guy overlooked. "Well, that was fun."

"She's a douche," Tara says, and I can't help but laugh. "She's jealous of you, Olivia." Her brow furrows. "I actually think there is more jealousy directed your way than you know."

"She has no reason to be jealous of me. Wait, what do you mean about jealousy directed my way?"

"Go look at yourself in the mirror. I mean really look. But it's more than that, Olivia. You're something very special. Inside and out. You just don't realize it."

I smile at Tara, feeling a little better. "Thank you."

"Those that do realize it are threatened by you."

Now it's my turn to frown because I have no idea what she's getting at.

"Okay, now go. Go flirt with lover boy."

I roll my eyes at her and stuff my notepad into my apron. "I don't flirt. I don't even know how."

"Just bend over a lot. No man can resist it when a woman aims her ass their way."

"Ohmigod, I am not doing that." She laughs and walks away, and before I take over her section, I run to the back office, grab my purse from my locker and pull out the foundation. I pour a generous amount on my finger and dab it on my face. I wince, but the sting reminds me of the way Jesse kissed my mouth, and body...between my legs. If I had to cover all my tender parts, I have to bathe in this stuff when I get home.

"Hey," Jesse says coming in behind me.

The door clicks shut and I turn quickly, recapping the bottle of makeup in my hand. He takes in my fingertips as I rub them together.

"Everything okay?" he asks, his eyes narrowing.

I point to my face. "Just covering up the evidence."

He laughs, and my God, the sound curls around my body and settles between my legs. "It's not like we committed a crime, Olivia, and we are supposed to be dating, right? Adults who date usually have sex."

"I know, but we're pretending."

"Yeah, maybe. But my cock clearly didn't get the memo." He steps up to me, grips my hips with both his hands and drags me closer. "I was hard as granite last night. There's no faking that." Heat invades my body as six feet of pure testosterone hovers over me. Dear God, I want him again.

"Yeah, you can't fake that," I say, and remind myself this is

Jesse, the guy I crushed on my whole life, and had sex with last night. I know he's simply helping me, but there's no denying he's turned on...by *me*. He made me feel beautiful and wanted, loving all my curves, and I have to say that is a complete mindfuck and sort of empowering.

"Yeah, my cock made it perfectly clear to both of us that he wanted in here." One hand leaves my hips and slides between my thighs. He touches me through my pants lightly, and my sex moistens.

I gulp. "Yeah, it did."

"It's sort of making it perfectly clear that he wants in here again." He takes my hand and presses it over his zipper. A tortured sound catches in his throat and my knees wobble when I feel how hard he is. Here I thought he'd be sated after last night. Then again, I'm not. All I can think about is having him inside me, pushing hard and deep and bringing me to climax. My nipples tighten, wanting that right now. How the hell am I going to get through this shift?

He dips inside my pants, and I gasp as he lightly strokes my clit. I clutch his shoulder, my gaze darting to the door. "We can't. Anyone can walk in on us."

He strokes me, gliding his finger over my clit, and his groan of delight thrills me. "I just needed to see if you were wet." He pulls his finger from my pants, and I stand there sexually frustrated, not knowing whether to be happy or not that he stopped.

"Hey, Boss," Angela says, the door flying open. I jump back, and Jesse turns, hiding me while I try to pull myself together. "Ah, was I interrupting?"

"What's up, Ang?"

"So, the rumor is true huh?" she says.

"Rumor?" Jesse asks.

"You two are a thing now. About time."

My God, why does everyone keep saying that? Jesse and I

are friends—friends with benefits now—and he's not looking for more than that. He's my best friend's ex, who is pretending to be my boyfriend to help me get another guy.

Could this be any more messed up?

"Yeah, we're a thing," he says. "Did you need something?" he asks, and redirects the conversation. He follows her out, and gives me a minute alone in the office to pull myself together. I apply more makeup, give myself a once over in the mirror and plaster on a smile.

By the time I make my way to the bar, it's hopping, the rush hour lunch crowd filling chairs and tables. I head to the pool tables to take orders.

Colin leans against the table, and crosses his feet. He's hot and sexy, there's no denying that, but he's no Jesse.

"What can I get for you guys?" I ask, and Colin grins at me.

"What?" I ask.

He shrugs. "Nothing."

"Beer?" I ask, and I get a round of nods from those playing.

"So, your boyfriend," Colin begins.

"What about him?"

"He beat me last night. Seems like he's beating me at a lot of things lately." He grins at me, and I get the sense that he's talking about me.

My God, was Tara right? Is Colin noticing me because I'm with Jesse? I'm not great at relationships, but that seems all kinds of wrong to me.

"Is that right? He never told me," I say.

"I guess you two had other things to talk about," he says, his gaze roaming my face. I flush at his inspection. I gulp. Does everyone know what Jesse and I did last night?

"I'll be back with those drinks," I say and scurry off, except I nearly trip on my feet in my hurry to get away. I resist the urge to look over my shoulder, but I can almost feel Colin's eyes drilling into my back. I reach the bar and put my tray down. Jesse is watching me very carefully.

"Everything okay?"

I smile. "Yes, four drafts for the guys," I say.

Jesse goes quiet as he fills the glasses and I place them on my tray. Uneasy silence arcs between us and wanting to break it, I say, "I hear you beat Colin at cards last night."

He wipes his hands on a rag and shrugs. "I can't let him win everything."

Why do I get the feeling that he's talking about me? I never felt like anyone's prize before.

"You'll have to put his money to good use," I say.

"Already did."

"Oh, what did you buy?" I ask.

"Check your locker."

Intrigued, I head back to the pool room and distribute the beer. I take a few food orders, drop them off to the kitchen and head to my locker. I open it and find a brand new pink backpack. My heart jumps into my throat. The door creaks behind me and I spin to find Jesse leaning against the doorjamb.

"Lucas said pink was your favorite."

I hug the backpack to my chest, as my heart misses a couple beats. "You guys did this?"

He nods. "Do you like it?"

"I love it, but you didn't have to do this." The man is thoughtful, sweet, and checks his gentleman card at the bedroom door. Talk about the perfect trifecta.

Careful, Olivia.

He pushes off the wall. "You watched Lucas for me, and I cleaned out Colin's wallet." He chuckles. "I thought the prize should go to you."

"This was so incredibly sweet. I don't know how to thank you."

"You're the sweet one, Liv," he says, his eyes so dark, so focused on my mouth, all the air leaves my lungs in a whoosh. "And I can think of a few ways to thank me," he says, his gaze leaving mine to take in his colossal desk. Is he thinking about bending me over that? Oh God, I hope so.

I sound like a squirrel jacked up on Red Bull when I say, "Well, you'll have to let me know what I can do."

His grin is wide, and wicked, and full of promise. "Oh, I will. As soon as your shift ends, I'll be sure to let you know."

My gaze is transfixed on her sweet ass as she sashays across the room and delivers drinks to the guys. Colin watches her carefully, like he's found a new appreciation for the girl who has been his friend since childhood. I like him, but if the dumb fuck couldn't see how amazing she was before, he doesn't deserve to have her now. I glare at him, and his gaze lifts, latches on mine like he can feel me staring. His head jerks back when I practically snarl at him, and he turns from me, going back to his game.

What the fuck am I doing?

I should want him to be looking at her, admiring her the same way I do. But for some reason it bothers me. I'd better get the hell over that. What Liv and I did in the bedroom last night was over the top, out of this world, and that's not just because I hadn't been with anyone in a long time. But I can't forget it's Colin who she really wants. It should be perfectly fine with me.

Should be, being the key words here.

Well, fuck.

Tara comes to the counter and hands her drink order over.

She's looking at me carefully, but I'm not up for any kind of interrogation from her. She's about to open her mouth when I cut her off.

"Can you get Jack's table set up for him?" I gesture with a nod to Olivia's father as he and Heidi enter.

"Sure thing, Boss," she says, and I don't miss the smirk on her face. The woman is too smart for her own good. But I suspect she'll keep her promise and not tell anyone we're just pretending.

I go back to making drinks, filling the dishwasher and polishing glasses. I try not to stare at Olivia when she stops at Jack's table. She makes her way back to me, a frown on her face.

"Everything okay?"

"Yeah, Dad said he was going to get a key made for me today, but he forgot." She wipes her tray with a rag. "I worry about him, sometimes."

"You worry about him *all* the time," I say.

She laughs. "True."

"He's a grown man, Olivia. He can take care of himself." Wasn't that what I just said to my grandmother? I'm beginning to wonder if that's true.

"I know, but...I worry about his memory." She snorts. "I worry about mine too."

"You should. You're the one who keeps losing her key."

We both laugh and Tara casts us a glance.

"I won't have to worry about that now that I have a lovely new pink backpack. That was so thoughtful."

"Yeah, it was," I tease. "But you're going to pay for it." I nod matter-of-factly, trying to pull a reaction out of her.

Never one to disappoint, her eyes go wide as her cheeks color. Does she have any idea how sexy it is when she goes all innocent like that? She opens her mouth and closes it.

"Something on your mind?" I ask as she struggles for her words.

"Actually, yes," she says. I angle my head, and go silent, handing her the floor. "I was wondering if you were going to bend me over your desk, or let me ride you in your chair."

What. The. Fuck.

I nearly swallow my tongue as she steps away, leaving me standing there with the boner of all boners, completely dumfounded, and aroused and fucked over...and... When I'm finally able to pull myself together, I shake my head and laugh. I guess I must have unleashed something in the good girl who always follows the rules and suddenly decided two could play my game.

Play we will.

I go back to pouring drinks, and the day couldn't drag on more. I've never been more anxious to close up shop. Thankfully it's Sunday and we lock up late afternoon, after the lunch crowd clears, giving the staff time to be with their families for Sunday dinner. I plan to eat with Lucas and Grandma right after I turn the sign to closed, but before I do...

Tara gives a wave as she heads out, and I glance around, my dick hardening when I find Olivia washing down the last table. I remove my apron, check the locks on all the doors and make my way to my office. Before she leaves, she has to collect her things, and I have to put my cock in her again.

I clear off the top of my desk, my mind fixated on... bending her over it. Is that what she wants or would she rather ride me in this chair? I laugh. I have no idea why I'm debating which way I want to take her when we can do both. When it comes to her, I have the stamina of a teen.

The door opens and her big doe eyes land on me. "Hi," she says quietly, closing the door behind her, and setting the lock. My dick jumps at the sound, and lets me know she's as into this as I am.

"We all locked up?" I ask, even though I checked the doors myself.

"Yeah, everyone is cleared out, it's just us."

"Good, because there is something important I need to talk to you about," I say, my voice so serious, her eyes narrow, that worry line on her forehead making an appearance.

"What is it?" she asks as she unties her apron, giving me a nice view of her curvy hips. Jesus, I want to sink my teeth into her voluptuous softness again.

I stand, shove the rest of the things on my desk to the floor, and say, "How exactly would you like me to take you first?"

Her eyes dim with desire, and her sweet nipples harden and poke against her bra. My mouth waters for a taste. I cross the room, slide my hand around her waist and drag her to me.

"When you say first, does that mean you want to do both those things I mentioned?"

Jesus, that mouth of hers. Sweet and saucy.

"That and so much more, Liv," I say, and push my cock against her stomach. "All the things you want to learn." She glances down, her brow furrowed. "Wait, are you too sore? I wasn't exactly gentle last night. Maybe I shouldn't have—"

"Oh, yes, you should have," she said, her boldness back in play.

"Then what's on your mind?"

"I want you here," she says, and takes my hand and puts it between her legs. "But I also want you here." She cups her breasts through her shirt and squeezes them and I nearly shoot a load off. "I've never done anything like that, and I want to try." I really did unleash something in her and I damn well love it.

"First, let me say I love that you're being so honest with me, and second, here's the deal," I say around a tight throat.

"We have lots of time to try everything you want to try before we stage a breakup."

"What about coming in my mouth?"

"Fuck," I blurt out and she tries to hide a chuckle. "You like this, don't you? You like fucking me over."

"I prefer it when you fuck me over."

"Okay, then." I grip her roughly, turn her around and put my hand on the back of her neck. With a little shove, I lower her onto my desk and her little cry tells me how much she loves when I go caveman on her.

She grips the desk, her nails clawing at the wood as I kick her legs open. I grip her hips for leverage, and push my cock against her sweet ass. I'm sure that's something else my neighbor has never tried.

"Can we dim the lights?" she asks, and it catches me off guard.

"If we do that, how am I going to see this sweet cunt of yours?" I ask, and the hard quiver that goes through her body strokes my cock.

"I'm just not all that comfortable with—"

"Babe," I begin. "All day I've been thinking about getting my hands and mouth on your body, and getting a better look at all these voluptuous curves," I say and run my hands over her hips and sweet ass. "I've barely been able to think. But if you want the lights off..."

Her throat works as she swallows, and that's when understanding dawns. This woman is fucking gorgeous. She might not be standard magazine thin, always stood in the shadows of her flamboyant and flirty friends who liked to steal the spotlight, Kylie included, but who the fuck wants that—and she better not have made Olivia feel less than perfect. Liv's innocent sensuality is a huge turn on, and I want to show her she's the hottest girl on the planet. I lean over her, put my mouth near her ear.

"You are the hottest fucking woman I know. I love your body, Liv. I'm going to worship every fucking inch of it with the lights on or lights off. Preferably lights on, but no pressure. Your call."

I run my hands over her back and she takes her time to answer. She finally breaks the quiet and says, "I kind of want to see you too."

Fuck yeah.

"They can stay on?"

"Okay," she says.

"Good, because it's going to be so fucking hot when I put my cock in you from behind like this, and see all your hot juices coat the length of me after I make you come." She gasps, a tremor going through her. "But first this."

I reach around her body, and release the button on her jeans. I tug them down, just enough to get my greedy hands on her sweet pussy. I touch her, and find her soaking wet. It blows my fucking mind.

"I'm guessing you've been thinking about me today, too."

"I have been," she whimpers and tries to buck against my hand. I pinch her clit, and her resulting moan rubs my dick. "I almost locked myself in here so I could touch myself."

I gulp air, and lean over and lift her, until her back is pressed against my chest. I turn her, grip her hips and set her on my desk. "I want you to show me."

Her eyes are a bit wide, unsure. "Don't go shy on me now, Liv. You want to experience everything, then you have to be open to everything."

"You're right," she said, and slides her hand between her legs, but I need them wider so I can see her finger in action.

I grip her pants, tug them down her legs and toss them away. My fingers bite into her thighs as I spread them, open her wide.

"Show me," I command in a soft voice.

She rubs her sweet clit, circling her finger around it, and bracing one arm. I rip into my pants, and shove them to my knees. She moans louder, encouraged by my words.

"Don't you dare come. I want my mouth on you for that."

Her hips lift, and she slides a finger inside her tight hole. I stroke my cock, and grunt at the sexy sight before me.

"That's it, just like that." I take in her closed eyes. "Open your eyes, babe, look at me." For some reason, I want her to know it's me in this room with her. I don't want her fantasizing about anyone else. Her eyes go wide when she sees me with my hand on my dick, and her lips part. She swipes her tongue over her parched lips, and my cock twitches to fuck her breasts and come down her throat.

All in good time.

She wiggles her sweet ass on my desk, leaving a burning imprint in my memory. I'll never be able to look at the damn thing again without thinking about this moment, how gorgeous she looks as she rides her fingers. I let her finger-fuck herself for a moment, then step back up to her. I take her hands, and flatten them against the desk. "They stay here now. Your orgasms are mine."

"Oh, God, Jesse."

I run my hands up her inner thighs, her heat scorching my flesh. "You're so close, babe," I say, and press the pad of my thumb to her clit. Her body quivers and she arches up to provide better access to her sweet spot.

I slide a finger into her and bend to take her clit into my mouth. I suck her deep, nibble on her engorged nub and one of her hands goes around my shoulder. She grips at my shirt, explores me with her fingers, squeezing my taut muscles as I take her higher and higher.

I want her hands on my body, but I'm not about to stop what I'm doing to remove my shirt. I lick her clit, lap at it with my tongue and slide another finger into her. She cries out my name and her fingers rake my skin through my shirt, and a second later she's coming all over my hand. She pulses around my finger, and I growl as her sweet taste floods my mouth. I drink her in, not wanting to miss a drop as her moans seep under my skin, and my cock thickens impossibly more.

Once I finish tasting her and her body settles from the pleasure, I drag her from the desk and set her on wobbly legs, ready to make her come for me again.

"You good?" I ask, when she quivers.

"So good," she murmurs, and I'm seconds from bending her over my desk when she drops to her knees. She takes my swollen cock into her and I watch her face, take in the fascination in her eyes. She's inexperienced, but the curious, excited way she's looking at my cock—like she's never really seen one up close and personal before—sends a thrill through me. Yeah, she had me in her mouth last night, but the lights were off.

"You like him?" I ask, and she lifts her chin to smile up at me.

"Leaving the lights on was a good call." She runs her fingers over me, tracing my thick veins. "You're so soft to the touch." She circles my crown, and bends forward to lap at the pre-come pooling on my head.

"Fuck, Liv, that feels good."

"What else do you like?" she asks.

"I like anything you do."

She slides a hand between my legs and captures my balls. "How does this feel?" She gives a little squeeze.

"Tighter," I instruct. She grips a little harder and chuckles when my cock jumps in front of her face. "Yeah, just like that."

She grips me by the base and runs her hand up and down the long length of me. "What about this?" she asks.

"Pull me toward you."

She does as I request, and I grip her hair and tug, needing to hang on. All I want is to bend her over and watch my cock slide in and out of her, but this...this is too damn good to stop. Besides, she wants to learn and that's what this is all about right?

She takes me into her mouth, and my hips instantly jerk forward, and I nearly gag her. I pull back, and she glances up at me.

"How can I take you deeper?"

Fuck me sideways.

"You don't have to do that."

She shrugs. "What if I want to?"

"Babe," I say and cup her cheek.

"Yeah."

"Relax your throat. If you do that, I can try to slide into it. If that's what you want."

"It is," she says.

"You like learning new things, huh?"

"I'm a good student, remember."

I do remember, and that thought reminds me she's leaving here in a couple of months. But I can't dwell on that right now, not when her mouth is on me again. Sweet baby Jesus, this woman can give head—whether she realizes it or not.

She bobs forward and once again she chokes, but she's not one to give up so easily. Her hands snake around me, and she cups my ass, pulling me into her hot mouth. After a few tries, her throat relaxes and I damn near lose my mind, when she takes me deep, deeper than I've ever been taken before.

I'm so hard and thick with desire, I'm not sure how I'll hang on. I grip her mess of hair, wrap it around my hand and rock into her, just a couple more pumps until I can get into her sweet pussy.

My cock aches for release, and with every ounce of

strength I possess, I tug on her hair, and pull her off my cock. She leans back, heat and anticipation in her eyes.

"Are you going to bend me over now?"

"Fuck yeah."

I pull her up to her full height, and plant my mouth on hers for a deep, hungry kiss as I slide a hand up her shirt and cup her breasts. She arches into my touch, and I remove one hand and put it on the back of her neck. I deepen the kiss, tangle our tongues, unable to get enough of her. She grinds against me, and I break the kiss, turn her around, and push her forward until she's splayed across my desk, her sweet ass poised my way. My chest against her back, I fall over her, and growl into her ear.

"I have never been so turned on in my life."

She whimpers. "Same."

I touch her ass, grab a fistful of her creamy lushness and squeeze. She wiggles and moans, and when I give her a little slap, she yelps. I chuckle as I bend over her and press my mouth to her back. Peppering her with kisses, I slide my hand between her legs, and slide two thick fingers into her dampness.

"You're soaked," I tell her. "So hot and ready for my cock."

"Please" she murmurs, and rubs her upper body against my desk. I'd love to have her completely naked, but taking her like this, with her shirt on and my pants barely off, comes with its own excitement. It's easy to tell she likes it too, and this is all for her.

Yeah, right.

This is for me too, and I'd be a fool if I didn't believe it.

I grab my cock, and run it over her sweet slit. She pushes back trying to get me inside when I come to an abrupt halt. The world suddenly closes in on me.

"Fuck," I murmur. "We can't do this."

She goes still for a second. "It's okay," she says, and when she tries to lift, I hold her down. "You're right, it's a bad idea."

"No, it's not a bad idea," I say, even though it is. "I want to do this, Liv. You have no fucking idea how much, but I don't have any condoms here."

The only audible sound is her heavy breath as she goes quiet, like she's considering that.

She takes a sharp intake of breath and blurts out, "I'm clean."

My heart lurches. Is she suggesting what I think she's suggesting? Would having sex without barriers—with her—be a good idea?

"I'm clean, too. But ah...kids. Maybe someday, but ah..." I say, even though I'm sure that will never happen, considering I have no time for that in my life and I'm pretty particular who I let into Lucas' life. "Are you on the pill?" I ask, and pray her answer is yes. I swear if I don't get inside her, something is going to rupture.

"No, but...."

"There are other things we can do, Liv."

"No. I want this and chances of me getting pregnant are slim to none."

My heart nearly stops. "Liv?" My God, why is this the first time I'm hearing about this? I'm about to ask when she speaks.

"I want you inside me," she says, her voice a pleading whisper. "Please, Jesse."

"I want that too." My cock rubs against her ass, and as sensations rocket through me, I struggle to think this through, to make the right decision.

"Please, Jesse," she begs again, and I put my cock at her opening and slide into her, burying myself deep. I groan as her sweet cunt grips me hard.

"Yes," she cries out and claws at the desk. I grip her ass

and jerk forward, going as deep as I possibly can. My eyes shut against the intense pleasure as it pours through my body. "So good."

I inch out, glance down at my wet cock, glistening in the overhead light, and feeling a little frenzied, drive back into her again. She rocks against the desk, her cries filling the room. I swallow, but control is a thing of the past. I push, hard blunt strokes meant to take her there quickly and when I reach around her and apply pressure to her clit, she breaks.

Her hot cum singes my bare flesh, as I rock into her. I grip her hips hard, my fingers biting into her curvy flesh, and as much as I want to prolong this, I can't. Heat bursts through me, and I seat myself high inside as I fill her with my hot cum.

"Jesse," she cries out. "That feels—"

"I know what it feels like," I say as I collapse on top of her.

"What?" she asks, obviously confused as I cut her off.

"It feels like more," I say, and lift her. I spin her around. "Now, what was it you said about riding me in my chair?"

11

OLIVIA

I steal a glance at Jesse as he drives me home. Honest to God, sex with him is incredibly hot and completely satisfying, yet I still want him again. Who knew underneath my sensible clothes a wild woman existed? I guess it took this man's touch to bring her to life. Now that she's alive, she's sort of ruling my head...and maybe my heart.

Ugh.

I can't go there. I won't.

"Liv."

"Yeah?"

"You're quiet." He casts me a glance. "Doing okay?"

"Just thinking."

"About?"

Oh, about how crazy I am for you, how I have to move shortly, and even if I didn't, we couldn't be together anyway. There are numerous reasons we can't be together, and the fact that he wants kids, and I can't have them, was just one more.

"Hey," he says, and reaches over to give my knee a squeeze. "What's on your mind?"

"Colin," I blurt out. I don't want him to get the wrong idea here. You know, that I might just be using Colin as an excuse to sleep with him. What would Jesse think of me if he ever found out now. Sure, we're both having fun, but honesty is important, to both of us.

"Right," he says. "I was thinking about Colin too."

"You got a crush on him?" I tease, anything to lighten the mood.

He gives a humorless chuckle. "If you're leaving in a couple of months, and you guys do end up together before that..." He puts both hands back on the steering wheel. "Have you given your distance any thought?"

"Actually, no," I say. It's the truth. I've not given any thought to being far away from Colin. From Jesse, yes. But not Colin. "I guess we cross that bridge when we get to it."

"Okay." He stares straight ahead, hits his signal, and pulls into my driveway.

"Thanks."

I'm about to reach for the handle, but he stops me. The dashboard light illuminates his face, as intense blue eyes full of questions lock on mine.

"Can I ask you a question?"

"Sure," I say, and brace myself. Does he know? Does he know I'm into him, and not Colin?

"You said you can't have kids. You never said anything like that to me before." I nod, and stare straight ahead. "If you don't want to talk about it, you don't have to. It just really took me by surprise."

"I found out a few years ago. I have very painful periods." He nods like he understands that. "I had some tests done and found out I have scarring in my tubes from endometriosis. Chances of me having children are pretty slim."

"I'm sorry," he says, his hand sliding across the seat to capture mine. "But there are other ways if you want children."

"Yeah, I know," I say lightly as my insides coil into a tight knot. "There's always in vitro, but it's costly, not a sure thing, and I kind of need a guy for that."

"True." He looks down, like he's giving it serious consideration. "You want kids, don't you?"

"I just sort of put the idea aside, you know. I have school, Dad. Those are my priorities right now, so I don't see it happening anytime soon, or maybe not ever."

"I understand."

He looks like he's about to say something else, but my throat is tight and I don't want to talk about me anymore. "What about you, Jesse? You said maybe someday you'd like to give Lucas a sibling."

"Yeah, and like you I don't see it happening anytime soon, or maybe not ever."

My heart squeezes, hurts for the man who lost so much and had given so much up. I hate that Kylie hurt him. Does he still love her? Does he hope one day she'll come back?

"You're not really on the market anymore," I say. "Lots of women are disappointed in that."

He chuckles. "You know I have to be careful."

"I do."

He rolls his shoulders, and while the movement is supposed to be relaxed, it's not. "It's going to take a special woman to put up with me."

"She'll be the lucky one. You and Lucas are amazing."

He swallows. "Not everyone thinks so."

"Do you...miss Kylie?" I ask, and take a breath.

"She left us. It was her choice. I'm not interested in having her back in my life, but it's not fair that Lucas doesn't have her in his. He has his challenges. Not every woman is up to those challenges."

"Yeah, I know." I take a breath, let it out slowly, and take in his profile. "The right woman is out there, Jesse. You just have to open your eyes and find her." He doesn't answer, he just stares ahead and nods. "Thanks for the lift," I say, and his hand goes to my shoulder. He toys with my hair.

He leans toward me and my lips tingle. "See you tomorrow."

"Yeah," I say, a bit breathless as his touch goes right through me.

"Seems so far away," he says and my heart hitches.

"Too far."

"I'm never going to look at my desk the same way," he says, lingering in my driveway like he's not ready to break the connection just yet.

I chuckle. "I can't believe we did that."

"Fun though, huh?"

"Yeah."

He glances at my house. "Your father is watching us."

"Probably wondering what's taking me so long to get his dinner up."

He laughs. "Yeah, or maybe he's waiting for me to kiss you. I guess we shouldn't disappoint him."

He leans closer, and his soft lips close over mine. One warm palm cups my cheek and I melt into him. His kisses are less hurried than earlier, less frenzied, but are just as deep and profound, seeping under my skin and curling around my heart. I moan into his mouth, but the sound snaps some sense back into me. We're having fun behind closed doors, but this tender kiss is just for show. I sigh inwardly.

This can't be real—for a million reasons.

I break the kiss and steal a glance at the window to see the curtain fall. "We definitely gave him a show."

"I don't think he'll be trying to set you up after that," Jesse says with a grin.

"I'd better go before he tries to cook and burns down the

kitchen." I swipe my tongue over my bottom lip. "See you tomorrow."

"Yeah, you will," he teases, and I get the sense that I'm going to be seeing a whole lot of him tomorrow—with the lights on.

It's crazy to think I agreed to that, but everything in his touches and kisses, the way he worshipped me, told me I had nothing to hide. This man likes all my jiggling parts, and makes me feel like the most beautiful woman in the world when I'm the sole focus of his attention.

I step into the house and Dad is whistling a tune as he flicks through the stations. His smile is big and wide when I walk into the room. He's happy, and I love seeing him happy. He deserves it, but I really hope this doesn't have anything to do with Jesse and me.

"Did you win at bingo this afternoon?" I ask.

"Nope. Didn't go. Decided to go tonight instead."

"Why are you so happy?"

"Can't a man be happy?"

"Sure. Did you happened to get out and get me a key made?"

He frowns. "Ah, forgot. Sorry."

Once again, I worry about his memory and health. "Are you hungry?"

He rubs his stomach. "Always."

I had put a pot roast in the crock pot before heading to work, so now all I have to do is cut the vegetables. "About thirty minutes, okay?"

"Need any help?"

"Nope, I'm good, thanks." I make a move to go, but stop when he raises his brow at me. "What?"

He turns the volume down on the TV. "You and Jesse, you're pretty hot and heavy, huh?"

Oh, God, I do not want to discuss my sex life with my

father. "Hot and heavy? What's that supposed to mean?" He's grinning from ear-to-ear, and I suddenly decide I don't want to know. I hold my hand up. "Never mind."

I head into the kitchen, but footsteps behind me let me know he's not about to let it go. A part of me wants to tell him the truth, but honestly, he seems so happy about me 'finding' someone. How is he going to feel when I fake a breakup?

"You plan to keep it long distance?" he asks. "Long flight back and forth between California and Boston."

I pull the vegetables from the fridge and grab the cutting board. "We haven't really thought that far ahead."

"Did you secure an apartment near Stanford yet?"

"It's on my list of things to do," I tell him. "I have been looking online."

"The clock is ticking," he says, and I realize that. I have to fly out there and secure a place for Dad and I to live. I've just been so busy, I haven't had the chance.

Is that the real reason, Olivia?

"Speaking of the clock ticking. What time is Heidi coming to get you tonight for bingo?"

He snickers at my attempt to change the subject as he seats himself at the island. "After dinner. Shame that boy didn't go to med school like he wanted. It's what his folks would have wanted, you know."

I nod and reach for the vegetable peeler. "I think so too, but he's a grown man who makes his own decisions and it's not my business."

"Seems like it is now, you know, with you two being all hot and heavy."

I point a carrot at him. "Can you please stop saying hot and heavy. We're dating, that's it, and you need to stop spying on us."

"I thought we were having an earthquake when you two

kissed. Thought I felt the ground shake." He chuckles. "Haven't seen that kind of chemistry since your mom and me."

I smile at Dad. I barely remember my mother, just a few fleeting images from when I was a toddler. He's been alone for so long. I'd love to see him have a relationship with Heidi—that would take his mind off me—but alas, they're only friends, and how can he start something if we're moving away soon?

"Maybe it's time he thought about selling the bar, and going back to school. The money would go a long way at Harvard. Or better yet, he could keep the bar and hire someone else to take care of it."

"Not my business, Dad."

"Phooey, it isn't." He waves gnarled fingers at me. "You two have been friends since you were in diapers."

"Doesn't matter."

"Well, it wouldn't hurt you to drop some hints, or maybe even pick him up a brochure or something." He taps his fingers on the counter, a scheming look in his eyes. "You know..."

I chop the carrots and drop them into a pot. Dad fishes a chunk out and bites into it. "I don't think I want to hear this."

"Harvard has a great human resource management program, and you've already been accepted. Maybe you two wouldn't have to deal with a long-distance relationship."

"Dad, my dream is Stanford. You know that," I say. I don't want to let him know a big part of my decision is so he can get to a better climate. If he thought I was making decisions based on his well-being, he'd never forgive me. But he single-handedly took care of me my whole life and now it's my turn to be there for him, make his life a little easier.

"Yeah, well, I'm just saying."

"You've said a lot," I tease, yet I can't help but think maybe he's right where Jesse is concerned. Maybe he does need a push in the right direction. Lucas is getting older, in school now, and Jesse's grandmother is always there to lend a helping hand. I could also... Wait. I won't be here to help. Heaviness settles in the pit of my stomach. I won't be around to give Jesse or Lucas a hand. If I went to Harvard...

What the hell am I saying? I can't just switch schools like that. I have my father to take care of.

But who's taking care of Jesse and Lucas?

My phone pings, alerting me to an incoming text, and I fish it from my purse. I take one look at the message, and nearly swallow my tongue.

"You've got to be kidding me?"

12

JESSE

With his backpack on his back, and his headphones dangling around his neck, Lucas stares wide-eyed at all the dinosaurs on display at the museum. I glance at Olivia as she follows along.

"Having fun?" I ask and nudge her playfully.

"Actually, it's very educational."

"It was good of you to come along. Lucas likes spending time with you."

"I want to spend as much time with him as possible before I move."

I stiffen at the reminder, but put on a happy face. "I'm glad you're making your dreams come true," I say my heart tightening. I hate to see her go, but I understand her needing to live her life and follow her path. For the last week, she's been in my arms every day, and I love being with her. A lot. There are times I even wonder if we could make a go of it, but no way would I ever ask her to stay and grow to resent me. Been there, done that. Besides, it's not like it's me she wants anyway. And I can't forget that she's been acting a bit strange this week. She acts like she wants to tell me something—something serious—then never does. Maybe she wants to stage the breakup?

Her smile falls. "What about you, Jesse? Have you thought about the future, and maybe following your dreams?"

I turn from her. "It's not my priority right now."

"Is it something you still think about?" she asks.

Could this be what she's been wanting to talk to me about?

"I do," I admit honestly. "Just having Lucas, and raising him alone has changed everything. Plus, I have the bar."

"Lucas will be in school. You'll have more time, and as far as the bar goes, you could hire a manager."

"Yeah," I say, my gut tightening as my thoughts go to my folks. They wanted me to go to med school, but what about the bar? Would I be letting them down if I stepped back, or sold it? They loved the place.

They loved you too.

As though reading my thoughts, she says, "Your parents would want you to follow your dreams, Jesse. They'd want you to be happy."

"Who says I'm not happy?" I might not have much of a social life, but I have my son and work and I am happy. Right?

"I'm just saying maybe it's time to think about it."

I look at her. Why the heck is she pushing this. Before I can ask, Lucas calls me, and I turn my attention to him.

"Daddy." He holds his hands up and growls. "T-Rex."

I pull my phone out, crouch down, and snap a picture of my son in front of the dinosaur, just as a crowd of kids all run in, wearing the same shirts, from some local camp. They're rambunctious and excited, and I'm about to jump up and rush to Lucas, when Olivia gets there first. She pulls him into the circle of her arms, protecting him from the commotion and secures his headphones. My heart races, and I stand still for a second, waiting to see if the disruption is going to be too much for him.

Olivia casts a quick glance at me and I relax and mouth the words, "Thank you."

She smiles and guides Lucas away, and we step into the next room, where there is less of a crowd. My sweet neighbor begins to talk to Lucas, distracting him from the crowd and talking about the flying dinosaur display.

Lucas stands there fascinated as the dinosaurs swirl about overhead, and after he's looked his fill, we move on to the next. Soon enough, we make our way to the gift shop, and I purchase a few toy dinosaurs for Lucas, not that he needs any more. We head out into the warm sunshine as Lucas' dinosaurs fight each other.

"Can we have sandwiches now?" he asks.

I ruffle his hair. "You bet, kiddo. I'm starving."

Lucas walks ahead of us and talks to his dinosaurs, and I fall into step with Olivia. "That was a close one. Thanks for jumping in."

"Of course."

Our knuckles brush, and heat goes through my body. Her phone buzzes in her purse, a personalized sound, and her entire body goes stiff.

"Whoa, everything okay?"

We move around a man and his dog coming our way, and I call out to Lucas as he starts getting a bit ahead of us. "Slow down, kiddo." I turn back to Olivia as her phone continues to buzz. "You going to check that?"

"No," she says quickly, too quickly and that's when I get a clue.

"Shit, is it Colin?"

"No, no," she says and shakes her head fast. "Why would Colin be texting me?"

"Because you like him."

"But he thinks we're together."

"He's been noticing you, Liv." I try not to clench down on my jaw when I recall the way his eyes followed her around the bar the other night. "If you want to stage the breakup—"

"I have to tell you something," she blurts out.

"Okay."

She takes her phone from her purse, and shows it to me. My heart stops beating as I look at the screen and read, Kylie. So, this is what Olivia's been hiding from me? She's been messaging Kylie.

"You've been in touch?"

"She texted last weekend, after...you know, on your desk."

"You didn't want to tell me?" My thoughts race. Is this why she's been asking about med school? Kylie left when I bailed and didn't live up to her expectations. Is this Olivia's way of trying to get us back together?

"I didn't want to upset you."

I scrub my face. "Why now? What does she want?"

"I don't know, Jesse. I haven't heard from her in ages, and she just texted out of the blue." She shoves the phone back into her purse. "She wanted to know what was new."

"What did you tell her?"

"I didn't."

Lucas makes his way into the busy park and we follow him. He stops to stare at a squirrel darting up a tree. Once it disappears into the leaves, he continues, making his way to his favorite spot on the grass. A duck crosses in front of him, and he laughs at it.

"Why the hell now, after all this time?" I take in the worried look in Olivia's eyes. "Are you going to answer her?"

"I don't know." She rolls one shoulder. "What do I even say?"

"Maybe she's trying to see if you're still friends."

"We're not," she says quickly and turns to see Lucas squat on the grass, and dump the contents of his backpack.

"Look, Liv. What she did to us—"

"Affects me too, Jesse. How could I possibly be friends with someone who could just walk away from her family?"

I swallow. "Yeah," is all I say.

"I don't want to talk to her."

"Then don't."

"I just wonder why...after all this time."

"Yeah, I wonder too."

"Here, Daddy," Lucas says and holds out a sandwich, but I've lost my appetite. I drop down and sit cross legged beside him. Olivia mimics my position and puts on a happy face, but it's easy to tell she's disturbed by the messages. What would I do if Kylie suddenly shows up, wanting back into our lives? How would it affect Lucas?

"Lucas, did you make these?" Olivia asks, her eyes wide as she bites into the sandwich and it brings a smile to my face. We exchange a look, one that says we're going to put Kylie out of our minds and enjoy this beautiful afternoon. She's a good sport. I totally love that about her. Actually, I love a lot about her. Too much.

Fuck.

Lucas beams up at her. "Daddy helped."

I hold my hands up, palms out. "All I did was lay out the bread."

"This is the best peanut butter sandwich ever," she says, and Lucas hands her a juice box. She pokes the straw in, and Lucas lays on his stomach, playing with his new toys as he eats. I get an ache in my chest as I watch him, when I realize how nice this is, picnicking on a Saturday with two of my favorite people. A guy could get used to this.

But this guy shouldn't get used to this.

"It goes in your mouth, Jesse," Olivia teases and reaches

for the side of my face. Her hand brushes my cheek, and without thinking, I bring her hand to my mouth and kiss it. Her eyes go wide and she takes a quick breath, her gaze sliding to my son, who is so enamored with his toys he's not paying us any attention.

I let her hand go, and she pulls it back, and I love that flush on her cheek, love knowing I can put it there from a simple touch. A dog barks, and I turn. I sit up a bit straighter.

"What?" Olivia asks.

I lower my voice. "That's Janice, Madelyn's mother." I point to Lucas. "The one who called him a not so nice name."

"Oh right." Olivia turns, and takes in mother and daughter as they play catch with their dog.

"I should go talk to her. Do you mind?"

"No, you should go."

I climb to my feet and Janice offers me a big smile when she sees me.

"Hey, long time," she says.

"How've you been, Janice?"

"Great," she says and looks at the grass where I'd been sitting. "I see you're dating again."

"No uh, Olivia is my neighbor, we go way back," I say, but it feels wrong introducing her like that when she's so much more to me.

She gives me a big smile and smooths her hair from her face. "Excuse the mess of me."

"Can I talk to you?"

"I hope it's to tell me you're interested in joining our support group. You know we'd love to have you."

"Thanks, but no, uh, it's about Madelyn," I say quietly, stepping closer so her daughter can't hear the exchange. I fill her in on what Olivia told me and I'm grateful that she takes the matter as seriously as I do.

She puts her hand on my arm before I go. "Thanks for

telling me, Jesse. I'll have a talk with her. You and I both know how hard it is to raise a child alone, and us parents need to stick together."

"Thanks, Janice."

"Stop over for a drink sometime. Bring Lucas."

"Uh, yeah sure," I say.

She drops to her knees to talk to her daughter as I make my way back to Olivia and Lucas, and Olivia is watching me carefully. She has a strange look on her face. Worry? Sadness? Jealousy?

Nah, I can't be right about that.

She crinkles her nose. "How did it go?"

"Good actually. Really good."

"Glad to hear that," she says and turns from me, just as a frisbee lands between us. Jacob, one of the firefighters who is a regular at the pub, comes racing over. Olivia picks up the frisbee and holds it out to him.

"Hey," he says. "I'm glad I ran into you guys. We need one more player for our team."

"I suck at frisbee," Olivia says.

"Colin is late, as usual." He snorts and grins down at me. "Up late again, I'm sure. If you know what I mean."

I get the gist as Olivia's eyes lift at the mention of Colin's name. Fuck, does she really want to be with a guy who's with a different woman every weekend? I mean, who he sleeps with and how many bed partners he has is his business and he's single, so he can do what he wants, but I'm starting to like the idea of her with him less and less.

"Why don't you go play, Jesse? You played ultimate frisbee in college, and Lucas and I are fine. Right, Lucas?" she says. Lucas growls his response, and Olivia stretches out on her belly to play dinosaurs with him. Lucas hands her one of his toys, and they play fight.

"Doesn't look like you two need me," I say and jump up. I

wipe grass from my jeans, and follow Jacob. We spread out, and spend the next half hour playing. We laugh and I actually feel a little lighter than I have in a long time. I kind of miss hanging out with the guys, and last weekend playing cards was fun. What I did afterward with Olivia was more fun, granted, and it's kind of weird. I liked knowing she was at my place, there when I arrived home. I think all this playing house is messing with me.

From the corner of my eye, I spot Olivia and Lucas walking to the pond, and Lucas is laughing at the quacking ducks. It brings a smile to my face. She's so good with him, and his heart is going to be broken when she leaves. But leave she must.

I jump, knock one of the players on the other team to his ass, and let loose a victory yell when I catch the frisbee and throw it to Callan Ward, one of the guys on my team. He's a good guy, a single dad like me, and often comes to support group. I catch sight of his little girl, blowing bubbles with Gemma, an old friend of ours, and from the way Callan keeps glancing at them, I wonder what's going on between the two. But the sight of Colin sauntering through the park, his eyes on my son and Olivia, instantly distracts me. Looking casual and relaxed, with his hands in his pockets, he walks up to them, and says something that makes Olivia laugh. She puts her hand on his chest, and gives him a shove, and he goes to his knee to talk to Lucas.

Possession.

Yeah, that's what I'm feeling right now. I force myself to turn my attention back to the game, just in time to get a frisbee in the eye. Shit that hurts. Jacob calls a time out, and comes to check on me.

"I'm good," I say. "Colin is here. I'd better get back to Olivia and Lucas."

"Colin, get your ass over here," Jacob says.

Colin stands, shoves his hands back in his pocket and comes our way. Olivia watches him walk away, or maybe it's me she's watching, walking to her.

Maybe that's just wishful thinking. Jesus Christ, I sound like a teenage girl.

"We winning?" Colin asks as we pass each other.

"Yeah, I scored."

He glances back over his shoulder at Olivia and snorts. "Yeah, you sure did."

13

OLIVIA

Inside Jesse's office, I untie my apron and shove it into my backpack. My gaze goes to his desk, and I instantly think of all the delicious things we did there. I run my finger over the wood, reliving the way he touched me with such deft hands, kissed me with such soft lips. A little sigh escapes my mouth as a fine shiver goes through me.

"Hey," Tara says, and I spin, so lost in thought I hadn't even heard her come in. "What's up with you and the desk? You in love with it or something?"

"Funny." She angles her head and stares at me like she has something on her mind. "What's up?"

She walks to her locker, reaches in and pulls out her purse. "Are you still going to Angela's wedding next Saturday?"

"Yeah, you?"

She nods and applies her lip balm. It's so dry in this place, even in summer our lips chap. "I assume you're going with Jesse."

That gives me pause. We haven't talked about it, but I supposed if we're still pretending to be a couple, it would be expected of us. "Yeah. Probably."

She recaps her lip balm and drops it into her purse. "Everyone will be there, Colin included."

I eye her. Okay, where is she going with this? When she doesn't continue, I tighten my ponytail and say, "And..."

She sits on the desk and kicks her legs out. "This might be a good time for you and Jesse to stage that breakup. Nice and public. It doesn't have to be nasty or dramatic or anything. Just a mutual parting of ways." My stomach squeezes tight, and I work to hide it. "Unless you don't want to." She grins at me, a knowing look on her face.

My heart jumps, my acting skills clearly lost on her. "Why wouldn't I want to?"

"Oh, I don't know." She puckers her lips like she's in deep thought and I'm not sure I want to know what she's thinking. "Maybe you're into Jesse now. You two seem hot and heavy."

"Hot and heavy." I roll my eyes, hard. "My God, have you been talking to my father?"

She laughs, and waves a hand. "Something like that."

"We are not hot and heavy. Please don't ever say that again." I toss my backpack over one shoulder, and try for casual. Like I'm not having the best sex of my life with the man I'm crazy about. "He's just doing me a favor."

In more ways than one, but she doesn't need to know that.

"Then you two might want to put a plan together, and then after the breakup, Colin can be the knight in shining armor and swoop in to be your rebound. The Park Plaza is a great place for you two to hook up. Lots of bedrooms right upstairs."

Oh, God, this is bad. So bad.

"I don't just jump into bed with guys, Tara."

"No?"

"No." I say. It took ten years before I jumped into bed with Jesse. Ten long years of watching him with other women, including my best friend, or rather former best friend. My stomach tightens. Why do I always feel like I'm doing some-thing wrong and deceitful when I think about her? Oh, maybe because she's the mother of Jesse's child.

"Well whether you do or not, it's a great place to stage the breakup."

"Yeah, you might be right." I glance down at my feet as I envision how that breakup will go. "I'll talk to Jesse about it."

She laughs. "I'm sure that'll make Brit happy."

"What's that supposed to mean?"

"Have you noticed she's been in a mood since she found out you two were together?" She gives an unladylike snort. "Like she ever had a chance with him, anyway."

My eyes narrow in on her as I consider that. "Do you think she wanted one?"

Tara shrugs. "I don't know, but she's been acting strange."

I don't like that. I don't like that at all. "Tara, do you think she stays in touch with Kylie?"

"No clue, why?"

I glance over my shoulder, and when I see that we're alone, I lower my voice and say, "Kylie started texting me right after Brit found out about Jesse and me."

"Whoa." She jumps from the desk. "Brit *is* a drama queen, so it wouldn't surprise me."

Is it possible that Kylie knows about Jesse and me and that's why she's reached out? We might not be friends anymore, but I'd never want to do anything to hurt her or anyone for that matter. She has no claims on Jesse, not anymore—I don't think, and Jesse did say he didn't want her back, but is that the truth? He's not moved on since she left. Oh shit, could he be waiting for her to come back? Oh God, maybe I never should have let this go so far. Kylie and I were good friends once, and I'm sure if she knew how I felt about Jesse back in the day, she never would have gone after him. And I can't forget if she does end up back in Jesse's life, she might try to break the connection Jesse and I have because I crossed a line.

But Jesse said we'd protect our friendship at all costs, right?

"I'd better get going," I say. "See you tomorrow." Needing to escape before she can see how rattled I am I make a beeline for the door and head outside. The late day sun shines down on me as I make my way home and birds chirp overhead, but not even the melodic sound can lighten my mood. I am in so over my head here. What was I thinking, agreeing to this? I wasn't, that's the problem. I pick up the pace and dash up the steps to my place, but when I dig into my backpack, my key is nowhere to be found. I dump the contents, but still can't find it.

"What the heck is going on?"

I knock on the door, but I'm sure Dad is still out with Heidi. He stopped by the bar earlier today for lunch and told me they were going to a few garage sales. It's his favorite thing to do on a Saturday afternoon. When my knocks go unanswered, I angle my head and spot Jesse's car in his driveway.

I stomp down the stairs, but honestly, it's no hardship spending time with him until Dad gets home. Last week, after the dinosaur show, we spent the night together and almost every night after that. After sex, we'd talk and sleep, but he never brought up med school again, and I really hope I didn't overstep any boundaries. I just want what is best for him. Just as he wants what's best for me—which is why he's pretending to be my boyfriend.

But what *is* best for me, and why am I suddenly starting to second guess my path?

I lift my hand to knock when the sound of a woman's laugh stills me. With my hand raised, I stiffen, and look through the window to find Jesse and Janice sitting at the table having coffee. Jealousy spears through me, and I swallow against a tight throat. But what right do I have to be jealous? He's not mine. We're pretending, and he's doing it for me. I take a step back, about to leave when Jesse glances my way. A smile splits his lip as he stands, and opens the door.

"Hey, come on in," he says. "Just getting off work?"

"Yeah, and I lost my key. Again."

"Are you serious?"

I nod. "I'm not sure what is going on. My bag was in my locker all day. I'm starting to think someone is messing with me."

"I'll talk to the staff tomorrow. See if they know anything or if anyone has been in the office who shouldn't be there."

"Thanks."

He turns, and says, "Olivia this is Janice, Madelyn's mother. Janice this is my neighbor, Olivia. You two might remember each other from the park."

I hold my hand out. "Nice to meet you, Janice. I hope I'm not interrupting anything," I say, but it's a lie. I hope I *am* interrupting them, and I hate myself for that. I want Jesse to be happy. I want him to find someone.

I want that someone to be me.

Oh, boy.

"I brought Madelyn over to apologize to Lucas, and invite him to her birthday party next month."

"Oh, how nice. I'm sure he will love that."

"Coffee?" Jesse asks.

"I'm good, thanks," I say and stand there feeling like a third wheel.

Madelyn lets out a squeal from the other room, and Janice glances at the clock. "Look at the time. I better get Madelyn home for her dinner, and let you get to yours."

"Thanks for stopping by." Jesse picks the empty mugs up

from the table and sets them in the sink. "I appreciate Madelyn apologizing to Lucas."

"I think they'll be great friends. We'll have to plan lots of play dates," she says, her eyes too bright, her smile too hopeful.

My God, why doesn't she just throw herself at him and end the misery?

"Sounds good," Jesse says.

My phone pings and I pull it from my bag as Janice gathers up her daughter and they all say goodbye at the door. I read the message from my Dad, letting me know he won't be home until late and to have dinner without him. I would, except I'm locked out. I don't want to ruin his day by having him come home to let me in, so I just tell him to have a good time. At least Kylie stopped texting. I mean, I'm glad she's okay, I was worried about her well-being like I would with anyone, but I have no idea what to say to her anymore.

I drop my phone back into my bag, as the door shuts and Lucas runs back into the living room to watch TV. I fold my arms and arch a brow when Jesse turns to me.

"She was lovely."

He grins at me. "You sound jealous."

Crap.

"Nope. Not at all. You should just know these playdates she's talking about aren't to get Madelyn and Lucas together."

"You don't think?"

"No." I poke him in the chest. "I think she's into you."

"Do you now?" he says and pulls me into his arms. "She can be into me all she wants, because later, after I put Lucas to bed, I'm going to be into you."

I note the reminder that what's between us is just sex. I plaster on a smile and will my stupid heart to stop aching. "I think I like the sound of that."

He presses his lips to mine. "Stay for dinner," he says, a

statement, not a question. "I'm going to throw some steaks on the grill." His mouth lingers on mine, neither of us in a hurry to break apart.

"Yum. I can whip us up a salad if you like."

"I like."

I'm about to move, when he reaches around, grabs a handful of my ass and gives a squeeze. He groans, then whacks me with his palm. "If you don't move, I'm going to be barbecuing with the world's biggest boner."

I chuckle and back up. "You're the one holding me here."

He puts his mouth to my ear, his warm breath trickles over my skin. "Because you're so fucking sexy."

I wiggle against his growing erection and he gives me another slap. "You're going to pay for that."

"That's the plan."

He laughs. "There's white wine in the fridge. I picked it up today. Your favorite."

I arch a brow. "Oh, it's like you knew I'd be coming over." I plant one hand on my hip. "Are you the key stealer, Jesse? Leaving me with no choice but to come over here, so you can have your way with me."

He grabs the lighter from the top shelf in his cabinet. "Shit, you're on to my wicked ways. Wait, does that mean I get to have my way with you later?"

I point. "Go light the barbecue."

"I'd rather light up you."

I shake my head and laugh. "Feed me first. It's been a long day."

"I'm on it." He disappears out the back patio and I pour a glass of wine and get to work on making us a salad. Once I'm done, Jesse calls out to me from the patio.

"Hey, Olivia, can you bring the steaks out?"

I pull the marinating steaks from the fridge, a cold beer for Jesse and refill my wine glass.

"Hey Lucas," I say as I pass through the living room. "What are you playing?" I ask when I see he has a controller in his hand, but he's so focused on his game he doesn't even hear me. My heart pinches as I watch him for a moment. How could a mother ever walk away from her child? How can I walk away from these two?

With that thought weighing me down, I step outside and hand the steaks and beer over and have a seat at the patio table. Jesse smiles at me and holds his beer up for a salute before taking a big drink.

"I love your backyard," I say. "It's so relaxing out here."

"We can eat outside tonight if you want."

"Oh, I want."

He goes quiet for a long time, and I stare at a squirrel dashing up a tree. Jesse finally breaks the quiet and asks, "What else do you want, Liv?"

I turn to him, and take in intense blue eyes as they stare at me. Do I dare tell him? Do I dare confess that it was *him* I wanted all along? What if I do and ruin everything between us? I'd rather have him in my life as a friend than not at all.

"Well," I say. "I've been thinking about Angela's wedding."

"Yeah."

"It might be a good time to stage the breakup," I say, and he turns from me, to flip the steaks.

His back is tight, and I hold my breath. Is it too much to hope that he doesn't want to, that he wants to make what we have here real? Even if he did, how could we make it work if I'm leaving? And of course, I can't forget that chances are slim to none that I can give his son a sibling, and that's not fair to either of them.

"Yeah, sure, if that's what you want," he says, his voice tight.

Tell him, Olivia.

Tell him it's not what you want.

His smile is in place when he turns to me. "You probably want as much time with Colin before you leave here at the end of the summer. You guys will have some things to figure out."

"Yeah," I say, and hope my voice doesn't come out as shaky as I feel.

"I'm going to grab another beer," he says. "Need a top up?" I shake my head and he disappears inside and I take a huge breath, grateful for the reprieve. I toy with my wine glass and work to pull myself together.

Jesse comes back with a beer, and plates. "So, this breakup," he says. "How do you want to go about it?"

"Something easy. We could just say we weren't compatible and the breakup was a mutual decision."

"Mutual, right," he says, and removes the steaks from the grill. "That means we have one week left to pretend, right?" He glances at me and I nod. "One week for me to do all the wicked things I want to do to you."

I gulp. "Yeah."

He nods. "Do you think that will be enough?" he asks, his back to me. For a second, I get the sense that he's asking something else altogether.

"Enough?"

He laughs and says, "You know, for me to teach you everything you want to know...in the bedroom."

"Right, yeah. I guess it will have to be," I say, even though I know this isn't about just sex for me, and one more week with this man will never be enough.

JESSE

I take a glance at the gorgeous woman beside me, as she watches the bride and groom exchange vows. My heart pinches at the dreamy look on her face. Is this what she wants from Colin? A guy to walk her down the aisle and give her the white picket fence? Perhaps the better question is, is Colin the guy who can give it to her? I'm having doubts on that. But if not him, then who?

You.

Shit, as soon as that one word pops into my head, I try to dispel it. We've been playing house, yes, and it's been fucking amazing, but she's leaving soon, for school and for her dad, and I refuse to be the guy to keep her from her dreams. No way am I about to tell her how I'm feeling and set either one of us up for that kind of future disappointment.

Her hand falls over mine, and I turn to her. Her smile is soft, warm, and water fills her vision. I lean into her, give her a little nudge. Hell, in a couple of hours, during the reception dance, I'm supposed to tell her this is over—even though I really don't want it to be.

You have no choice, dude.

Or do I?

No, no I don't.

The minister announces that Angie and Philip are now joined as one, and they begin to walk down the aisle. We all clap and follow them out, stopping to give hugs to the wedding party lined up in the hall of the magnificent downtown hotel.

"You look beautiful," I say to Angie, and she gives me a wink.

"Maybe you'll be standing up there next."

I laugh at that, but don't miss the way Olivia is watching the exchange with curiosity, and maybe even a little sadness. Is she worried that this will never happen with her and Colin, or is there something else going on in that brilliant brain of hers?

We all head to the dining area and find our seats. I read the place cards. Colin isn't seated with us, not that it's a surprise. Why would Angie put him at our table? She doesn't know it's him that Olivia really wants. I glance around and find him and Tara sitting awfully close. From my distance, I can't hear what they're saying, but the conversation seems awfully tense. What the heck? I hope Tara isn't spilling secrets.

I pull Olivia's seat out for her and she chuckles. "Such a gentleman."

I put my lips by her ear, forgetting that we're soon to break up and say, "Not always." Her body quivers beneath my mouth, and it vibrates through me. Energy arcs between us as we sit, and I wonder if the others in the room can feel the tension. Maybe I should get a room, and have one last night with her. Maybe that will finally douse the fire inside me.

Dinner is served, followed by wedding cake, and the longer the night goes on, the tighter my throat feels, and it has nothing to do with the tie around my neck. I take a glance at Olivia, who seems as uneasy as I do.

"Hey, you okay?" I ask.

"Yeah, the wedding was beautiful."

"You're beautiful," I blurt out without thinking, and take in the soft pink dress that highlights the tan on her face. A blush crawls up her neck. "What, you don't believe me? After all this time, you don't believe me?"

"Actually, Jesse. I do. You make me feel beautiful." She puts one hand on my chest, and her warmth goes through me. If we're so wrong, why does this...this...comfort and intimate familiarity between us feels so right. "No man has ever really done that before."

"Those guys are idiots."

She gives a humorless chuckle. "Not just guys. Lots of mean girls out there, too."

I stare at her. Kids and adults both can be cruel if you don't fall into a nice square box. I'm seeing that with my own son, and I'm working hard to change it.

"I'm sorry. People can be assholes." I remember the time in junior high when I sat with her during a particularly difficult time when those mean girls were picking on her.

"They can be."

"Any man in this room would be lucky to be sitting where I am right now. If they're too stupid to see how gorgeous you are, they're too stupid to have a chance with you."

She narrows her eyes. "Are you talking about Colin?"

Shit, I've said too much.

"No, I'm just saying," I say and glance at the bride and groom as they stand for their first song. But before the music begins, angels turns to the crowd.

"Tradition is for the groom to remove the garter and the bride to toss the bouquet before they leave for the night, but as many of you know, I'm not all that traditional." Cheers erupt from the crowd. She fist-pumps the air. "I plan to stay and shut this party down tonight." She grins at Phil and he kisses her.

Someone brings her a chair and she sits. Sexy music begins playing as Phil drops to his knees and fishes her garter out from under her dress—with his teeth. I laugh, glad that there are no children present. I can't even imagine Lucas' reaction. Good thing he's tucked in for the night with his great-grandmother. Phil finally gets the blue garter off, and swings it around his index finger.

Smiling back at the crowd, Angie lifts her arms. "So come on single ladies, someone is going to catch this bouquet and get this party started."

Chairs scrape as those in the crowd jump up, but Olivia doesn't move.

"Aren't you joining in?"

She shakes her head. "No, I don't...let's just let someone who is close to marriage catch it."

"You sure?"

She nods and looks back at the crowd. Angie scans the girls standing, and frowns when she sees Olivia still seated. Olivia rests back in her chair, and her hair is long and loose tonight, falling down her back. A light perfume scent fills my senses as she pushes a strand off her shoulder, and it's all I can do not to bend forward and press my lips to her neck, taste her one last time before she goes off with another man.

I briefly close my eyes, to get my shit together, and open them again when Olivia lets out a little yelp. Holy shit. She fumbles with the bouquet as it comes out of nowhere and hits her in the chest.

"I wasn't...I didn't..." she tries to say as everyone claps. "What the heck?"

"Looks like I'm stronger than I realized," Angie says with a laugh. "Get your ass up here, girl."

"Go," I say, and give her a nudge. She stands, and her dress falls, not quite reaching her knees. My God, she is so beautiful. She walks to the floor, and Angie puts her in the chair.

"What is going on?" she asks as Phillip twirls the garter in his hands.

"Well, whoever catches this garter has to put it on your leg, Olivia, it's tradition."

"I thought you weren't traditional," Olivia croaks out, her eyes wide. "Wait, who's putting the garter on me?"

"Here's where I'm going to show you that I'm not traditional," Angie says as she nudges Phil. He walks through the crowd, and I groan when he stops in front of me, palm open and garter waiting for me to claim it.

The crowd claps and when I catch Olivia's gaze, relief moves over her face. I guess she'd prefer me over a stranger sliding this up her leg.

"Let's go, Jesse," Phil says, and I push from the chair and shake my head. I scan the crowd as they cheer me on, and catch Colin's eyes. He has the strangest look on his face, and it feels like a fist to the gut. Putting this on her leg, while raunchy music plays and the crowd cheers us on, isn't conducive to our planned break up.

I drop to my knees in front of her. "You okay with this, Liv?"

"Thank God it's you," she says, and my heart beats a little faster. "It would have been so embarrassing."

Sweet, shy Olivia, who is anything but demure when I get her alone and put my hands on her.

"What is that music?" she asks, and shakes her head. I grin up at her.

"Want to give them a show?"

"Jesse...what are you up to?" I take her foot, remove her shoe and slip the garter over her ankle. I click my teeth together, playfully and give her a teasing wink. Her eyes go wide. "Don't you dare," she says, and I laugh. Putting it on with my teeth would be bad in so many ways, and I'd never do anything to embarrass her like that.

Maybe later, when we're alone, I'll use my teeth to take it off.

There is no later, dude.

Yeah, well, fuck that.

In a less-than-climatic mood for the crowd, I put the garter on, and lift her from her chair. Her body collides with mine and I slide my arm around her.

"Thank you," she says.

"Don't thank me yet."

Her body quakes beneath my touch, and I fucking love the way she reacts to my closeness. "What is that supposed to mean?" she asks, a bit breathless.

"Why don't you go find us a bottle of champagne and meet me in the lobby."

She angles her head, her eyes moving over my face like she's trying to figure out where I'm going with this.

"The night is still early, Liv, and I promise to make this worth your while." Yeah, if I couldn't make sliding the garter up her thigh a climatic event for her, I plan to make something else climatic. "Jesse..."

"Trust me?"

"Yes," she says quickly, without hesitation and it does the weirdest fucking things to me.

I put my mouth to her ear. "Five minutes. In the lobby."

She nods, and I give her elbow a squeeze to reassure her. She leaves my side and I make a beeline for the front lobby, quickly securing us a room. Five minutes later, she emerges from the ballroom, and her chest rises when she finds me near the elevators waiting for her.

With a bottle of champagne in her hands, she steps up to

me. "Are we celebrating something?" she asks as she holds the bottle up.

"I was thinking. If we have to end this tonight, why don't we go out with a bang?"

She swallows. "Do you think that's a good idea."

"No, it's a bad idea, and you and I both know how they go."

The doors open and we both step onto the elevator. I punch in our floor and our eyes meet during the short ride up. We stare at each other in silence, and there is enough tension to cut the air in the small space. The doors open and I put my hand on the small of her back to usher her off. Our steps are hurried as we make our way down the hall, and our knuckles brush, like we both need the contact.

Inside the room, I close the door and lock it. She's breathing so damn hard I'm worried she's going to hyperventilate. With my hands on her hips, I push her against the door, and put the champagne on the table beside us. My lips find hers for a slow, long deep kiss so steeped in passion, it sets my body on fire. Heat burns through me, my cock never more ready for anything, or...anyone.

"I need you naked. Need to be inside you, Liv." I wait for her consent, and when she nods, I slide my hands around her back and unzip her dress. She rolls her shoulders and I suck in a breath when the dress falls to her feet.

I stare at her, take pleasure in her matching bra and panties, and can't help but wonder if she wore them for me, that she might have hoped something like this would happen.

With confidence oozing off her, she cups her breasts, squeezes them together, and forms a tight little channel where my cock needs to go. I take a small step back and take off my jacket. I loosen my tie, and her body quivers when I wrap it around my hand, in much the same manner I'm going to wrap it around her wrists. We've done so many things over the last few weeks, but I've yet to tie her up, and goddammit, it's not because I want to teach her anything, it's because I fucking *want* her.

All to myself.

I remove the rest of my clothes, and take my dick into my hands as she continues to massage her full breasts. "Do you like that bra?" I ask.

"It's one of my favorites."

"Then you better take it off, before I rip it from your body."

She bites down on her lips, her excited little gasp curling around me. Five seconds later, her breasts spill free, and I bend to take her nipple into my mouth. I grip the tiny scrap of material of her panties that's keeping her sweet pussy from my mouth, and in one quick tug, I remove the lace from her hips.

"Were they your favorite, too?"

"Yes," she whispers. "But now you've ruined them."

I chuckle and take in the heat in her eyes. "You were never getting them back anyway, Liv."

"What is it with you and my panties?" she asks, her voice full of desire and amusement.

"Like you even have to ask." I drag her from the door, and cross the room, until we're standing by the bed. She sits and I toss my tie onto my pillow, and go to work on popping the champagne. I fill two glasses from the bar, and hand one to her.

She takes a drink and wets her lips. "Mmm, so good. I was parched."

I touch her shoulder. "Babe, I have a better way to quench your thirst." I nudge her and her excitement strokes my cock as she falls backward and cups her breasts, offering them up to me.

"Fuck yeah," I say, and while I might have checked my

gentlemanly side at the door, I plan to get her off first. I reposition her and flip her over until she's on her stomach.

"Ooh," she says as I put a pillow under her belly to lift her.

"I want you on my face," I tell her and go down on my back between her legs. I drag her to me until her sweet cunt is pressed against my mouth, and I suck on her clit.

"Jesse," she cries out, and bucks against my face. "Oh my God, that is so good."

She rides my face, wild, unabandoned, a woman who knows what she wants and has no problem taking it.

That's my girl.

I put my tongue inside her, rub her hot clit all over my wet face. Her breathing changes, and the second she starts whimpering, her release so damn close, I reach up, grab hold of her hips and drag her down my body until her legs are straddling my hips. Her eyes are wild, and she runs her nails over my chest, like she can barely hang on, but I want my cock in her sweet pussy when she feels that first sweet clench.

I lift her, and she holds her breasts, squeezing tightly as I lower her onto my cock.

"Yes," she cries out, her head going back as I fill her completely. Her hot wet cunt squeezes around me, and I growl with pleasure.

"Fuck me, babe," I say and she begins to move, lifting up and down and I hold her hips to help her. I power upward with her, wanting to bury myself balls-fucking-deep and knowing it will still never be deep enough.

"Jesse," she whimpers, a new urgency in her tone as she puts her hand between her legs, shamelessly rubbing her clit. I damn near shoot off.

"You are so hot, Liv. I love...this between us," I say, dangerously close to telling her all my secrets. What would she do if I did? What would she do if I said I never wanted this to end?

She rolls her hips and grinds down on me, and I can barely take this sexy sight of her. I reach for her hands, weave them in mine and her eyes flash to mine. As our eyes collide, warmth and intimacy passes between us, and an overwhelming amount of happiness—something I haven't felt in far too long—fills my soul. Sex with her, everything with her, is genuine and real, and so damn right. Sometimes I think I must be dreaming.

"Liv," I say.

"I know," she whispers, like she's feeling this every bit as much as I am. "Jesse, I'm there." She lifts and slides down the length of me, her muscles milking my cock as she gives in to the pleasure. Her body convulses and her hot juices pour down my shaft and tickle my balls.

"Fuck," I cry out and keep my dick inside her as she moves and writhes and just takes what she needs. After a big contented sigh, she grins at me and I grin back, the connection between us so goddamn powerful, I feel it deep in my chest, right around the vicinity of my heart. I grab hold of her hips and lift her from my cock and set her on the bed.

She frowns. "Jesse, what about you?"

"On your back. Hands on these gorgeous tits," I command in a soft voice and she squeals, knowing exactly where I'm going with this. I moan as she presents her body like a buffet and goddammit, I plan to take my fill.

She cups her breasts, forming a beautiful tight channel for my cock, and I squeeze my shaft, letting my pre-cum pool on her tits. I reposition and put my cock between her lush breasts and power forward. Her mouth parts, and she laps at my wet crown when I reach her mouth.

"Fuck yeah, you are sexy," I say, and she moans and squirms beneath me, massaging my dick in mind fucking ways. I pump against her body, and her sweet tongue treats me to a hot lick every time I reach her mouth. I want to be in her throat, but this... this is so goddamn good there is no way I could stop even if I wanted to. I fuck her, long and deep and so needy, my vision goes fuzzy around the edges. I pump once, then twice, and when I throw my head back, she knows my every movement and facial feature so well, she knows I'm going to come. She lifts up and opens her mouth for me, and her moan of pleasure wraps around me and squeezes tight.

I am so fucking in love with this woman.

I deplete myself, and her eyes are full of desire and wonderment as I fall beside her and drag her to my body. She rests her head on my chest, and I stroke her hair and arm, both of us lost in our thoughts for a long time. The air chills and I pull the blankets up. Minutes tick by for a long time, and for a second I wonder if she's asleep but then she runs her finger around my nipple, going lower and lower, teasing the hair from my belly button to my cock—which suddenly wakes up again. Something tells me this was her plan all along. Like me, maybe she just can't get enough. I harden and she moans and wraps her fingers around me.

I might have just fucked her, but I still need more. Yeah, she really does make me feel like a hormonal teen. I flip her back over and put her hands above her head, taking my tie to bind them together.

"Oh my God," she murmurs and wiggles. The knot is loose enough for her to get out if she wants, but I don't think she does.

I crawl back between her legs and crouch. I lightly pet her sex. "Such a pretty pussy." I say, and she swallows. "I think I'm going to need my cock in here again. Can you take me, Liv?"

"Yes," she says quickly, her body flushing.

I take my cock in my hand, and stroke until I'm hard as

steel. She widens her legs, opening herself up to me. I fall over her, and ease into her heat. I move my hips slowly, savoring the sweet feel of her body as I slowly make love to her. We move together slowly, each taking and giving as we savor the sweet, tender moment between us. In no time at all, she comes around my cock, and pulls another orgasm from me. Sated, I fall to her side again and release her hands.

She rests her head on my chest, the satisfaction in her eyes filling me with pride as she glances up at me, like she might want more than just sex. But how can I open up and ask for that?

How can I not?

I don't want to hurt her, or have any sort of resentment between us, but how can I just let her go from my life, from Lucas'? She's been open and honest with me all along, and doesn't she deserve the same from me? Honestly, if she was into Colin, wouldn't she have stayed downstairs and demanded we stage a breakup instead of hurrying to this room with me.

We need to talk, and we need to do it now.

"Olivia," I say and her head lifts from my chest.

"Yeah." She blinks dark lashes over brown eyes that gaze up at me with admiration, and something else...

Could it be love?

I open my mouth, about to come clean when my cell phone rings, my grandmother's special ring.

Shit.

15

OLIVIA

It's been a long week helping Jesse with a sick child. We left the wedding right after we found out Lucas had come down with chicken pox, and the next morning Jesse got a call from Janice, telling her Madelyn had them too, which is likely where he picked them up in the first place.

I hate that Lucas contracted the disease—and he's been itchy and achy—and I'm probably going to hell for being grateful that phone call ended our night, and we never did get to stage that breakup. Honestly, after sexy times, or rather, making love to Jesse—at least that's what it felt like to me—I never wanted to go downstairs and split up, or entice Colin in any way. It was a stupid, stupid plan.

Jesse and I both had chicken pox as children, but I've been keeping Dad away. He has a compromised immune system and he hasn't had the shingles shot, and so I don't want him catching anything. This morning I have to take him for his check-up, and then I have a late shift at the bar. All I want to do is sleep, but I'm not about to abandon Jesse and leave him short-staffed when he's home taking care of his son.

"All set?" I ask my father and put on a smile when he walks into the kitchen.

His eyes narrow. "You haven't been getting enough sleep," he says as he looks me over.

"I know. I'll sleep tonight," I say and brush it off. "After the late shift."

He grumbles something about Heidi driving him, but I put my hand up to stop him. "I'm your daughter, I'll drive you. Besides, Jesse lent me his car. He's home with Lucas and said he doesn't need it today."

"You both do enough for me as it is," he grumbles as we head outdoors, and I grab my key off the counter, lock up and drop it into my backpack. "I better not lose this one," I mumble.

"What's that?" Dad asks as I carefully zip up my new pink bag. My heart wobbles to think Jesse and Lucas picked this out for me.

"I keep losing my keys, or someone keeps stealing them."

His bushy brows collide as he frowns at me. "Now why would anyone want to steal your key?"

"No idea," I say and follow him down the stairs to the car. It's not like we really have any valuables, and no one has attempted to break in. "I guess it does sound kind of crazy." Or maybe I'm the crazy one. So preoccupied with my neighbor and future, I have no idea if I'm coming or going anymore.

I carefully back out of the driveway, and glance at Jesse's place as we head to Dad's appointment. I adjust the radio to my favorite station, and turn it down a bit.

"Have you given any more thought about Harvard?" Dad asks, as I pull into traffic.

I shrug, not sure if he's talking about me or Jesse, and take a left at the corner. A few minutes later, as I drive by Burgers and Brews, I spot Tara and Colin in deep conversation beside his car. I'm beginning to wonder if the two are hooking up, but Tara isn't one to hone in on anyone's man. She knows I *like* Colin and she's the one who put this ridiculous plan into motion.

"I don't know, Dad," I say. One of my biggest goals is to get him to a better climate. I cast him a glance. "How do you feel about moving?"

He always told me he was good with any decision I made, but now I'm beginning to second guess that. Why is he pushing Harvard all of a sudden? Is this his way of keeping Jesse and me together? He's willing to sacrifice his health for me? God, I feel so bad that I've been keeping the truth from him.

"I want what you want, kiddo," he says, and an uneasy feeling grows in my belly. I'm not sure I can ever have what I want, and if I move, am I taking Dad away from a place he really wants to be? He's always so vague when I ask him. He wants the decision to be mine, but a little bit of input would be nice.

A short while later, I pull into the clinic's driveway. I'm about to go in with him, but he waves me away.

"Go for a walk, and get a coffee. You look like you can use it. I'm fine on my own. I'll text you when I'm done."

I nod. He's a grown man, and likes to do things on his own when he can. Plus, he deserves his privacy, just like I deserve mine in certain matters, like online dating. I still can't believe he went ahead and did that without my permission.

"Sounds like a plan, actually." I stifle a yawn. "I could use a cup." I glance up and down the street and seek out the closest coffee shop.

"I shouldn't be too long," he informs me and makes his way toward the door. Once he disappears inside, I turn and begin a trek down the sidewalk. I pass by the Massachusetts College of Art and Design, and study the building and people milling about. I continue on a little more until I come to the medical school's admissions office and my steps pause.

I stand there for a long moment. Would grabbing literature on the program for Jesse be overstepping my boundaries? Then again, could a little nudge be such a bad thing? If he doesn't make a move soon, it's going to be too late for him, and life is freaking short, Jesse and I both know that. One minute a person is here, the next they aren't. I never want to see him look back one day and regret never having chased his dreams.

Am I chasing mine?

I turn my thoughts back to the man I'm in love with. It won't be easy pursuing a medical degree when you're a full-time father running a business, but maybe it's time he revaluated his life and nailed down what was important for his future.

"Oh, what can it hurt?" I mumble to myself and make my way inside. About twenty minutes later, armed with literature that Jesse could easily have gotten online, but might never have, I grab a coffee and trek back to the car. I sit inside and look over the information as I wait for Dad, but as I do, I consider my future.

Do I really want to move to California?

If I don't, what would it mean for Dad?

What would it mean for Jesse and me?

My heart beats a little faster as I run numerous scenarios through my rattled brain. Mainly, if I told Jesse how I felt, and he didn't feel the same way, what would that mean for our friendship? But how can I move to the other side of the country and continue to wonder, what if? But what about children...

Jesus, could this be any more complicated.

I tap on the steering wheel, and work to wipe the worry from my brain as Dad walks down the steps and makes his way toward me. I tuck the information into my backpack and toss it into the back seat. Dad is singing a tune as he climbs into the passenger seat.

"Sounds like it was a good visit."

He winks at me. "I might not be ready to run the Boston Marathon, but I can make it to paint night at the pub tonight."

I grin, my heart full of gratitude that he's doing so much better. I don't know what I would have done if I'd lost him too.

I can't lose Jesse.

With that thought bouncing around inside my brain, I drive Dad home. Once he's settled in the house, I change my clothes, and put Jesse's car back in his driveway. I dart up his stairs, and knock on his door. Just barging in doesn't seem right, even though he told me I never have to knock. He's a single guy, what if I walked in on him with...someone?

Okay, now where did that thought come from? I work to push down the lump rising in my throat when he opens the door, looking so sexy in nothing but his jeans, I resist the urge to throw myself at him.

"Hey," he says, as I hand over his keys. His eyes go wide in surprise.

"What?" I ask.

"You didn't lose them?"

"Funny guy." He slides his arm around my waist and drags me to him. His warm body heat seeps under my skin. My hands land on his broad shoulders, and I give a little squeeze. "Apparently, it's only my house key I lose."

"Which you do on purpose."

I lift my chin. "Excuse me?"

"Come on, stop denying it." He dips his head, his mouth inches from mine. "You keep losing it so you can come over here just to get ravished."

I'd have been tossing my key away for years if I had known it meant getting touched and kissed all over by Jesse. "As nice as that sounds…" I crinkle my nose. "I have a shift at the pub."

"Yeah, I know."

I'm about to pull away when he presses those soft lips of his to mine. I kiss him back, momentarily forgetting we're standing in his open doorway, for all the world to see. We stay embraced for a long moment, and a couple cars go by, slowing to watch the spectacle we're making of ourselves, no doubt. I expect someone to open their window and tell us to get a room already.

I'm breathless and giddy by the time we break apart. "How am I supposed to make it through the day after a kiss like that?" I ask.

"By thinking about what I'm going to do to you when you return."

I try to see over his shoulder. "How is Lucas?"

"Much better. We're both going crazy in here. He's no longer contagious, so I thought we'd go out, go to the park and maybe visit Grandma. She's missing us."

"I can imagine." I glance at the next car going by. "I'd better go."

"I can drive you." He jerks his thumb over his shoulder. "Won't take me long to get Lucas ready."

"Nope, I need the exercise."

"Hardly, you're perfect."

I go up on my toes and kiss him. When I break free, he angles his head, and studies my face. "What was that for?"

"For being you," I say.

"Oh," he opens his mouth like he wants to say more, but Lucas calls out to him from the other room.

"I'd better go," I say. "Have a great afternoon, and get some sun."

"Yeah, listen," he says and takes a strand of my hair, all humor gone from his handsome face. The blue in his eyes darken when they latch on mine. "There's something I'd like to talk to you about tonight."

"Actually," I say, thinking about the brochures in my backpack. "There's something I'd like to talk to you about." We both stand there for a moment, our eyes locked, our bodies brushing. Lucas calls for his father again, and I dash down the stairs.

"See you tonight."

"Hey Lucas, what's up?" he asks as his door clicks shut. I move down the sidewalk, and the hairs on the back of my neck stand. I glance over my shoulder the strangest sensation that someone is watching me washes over my skin. The hairs on the back of my neck stand up and I catch a flash of a woman before she disappears from my sight.

Wait, was that...?

16

JESSE

"Ready, buddy?" I ask, as Lucas secures his headphones around his neck.

I put his backpack around his shoulder as he gives me a nod. I grin at his too-long hair and press my hand to his forehead again, just to ensure there is no fever. It broke days ago, but I can be overprotective at times, and the last thing I want to do is bring anything to my grandmother's, even though she told me she had chicken pox and the vaccine for shingles.

With dinosaurs in both hands, Lucas heads toward the front door. He flings it open, and my heart jumps into my throat—wishing I'd gotten there first—when I see who is standing there, ready to knock.

"Why hello," Kylie says, and my first instinct is to protect Lucas. He pays her no attention as he plays with his toys. I carefully put him behind me, placing myself in between him and his mother.

"Daddy, I want to go," he says, a bit whiny.

"We will, kiddo. Just a minute, okay?"

"I want to go now."

I turn and put my hands on my son's shoulders. He's been cooped up all week, I get it, but I have a situation I need to deal with first. One I don't want him to know anything about. Not yet anyway.

"Just a second okay, bud. Then we'll go see Grandma, and have ice cream."

That seems to satisfy him for a moment as he grumbles some response, and I stand, running my agitated hands through my hair as I square off against my ex. A little warning would have been nice, but this is just like her.

"Did I catch you at a bad time?"

"Yes," I say through clenched teeth.

"Do you mind if I come in?"

"We're on our way out." I grip the doorframe and squeeze. "You can't just show up here like this, Kylie. It's not good for Lucas."

She purses her lips. "What about you, Jesse? Is it good for you?"

Wow, seriously?

She puts her hand on my chest and I remove it. Her smile turns venomous. "What do you want?"

"I thought we could talk." Lucas makes a noise. "I want to see my son."

"A bit late for that, don't you think?" I ask, lowering my voice.

"He's my son, Jesse."

"Please don't do this, Kylie," I say, not wanting this situation to escalate in front of Lucas. "Not here, not like this."

"Daddy, I want to go," Lucas whines.

"Can we talk later? I'm taking him to my grandmother's. I can meet you afterward." No way am I about to let her just walk back into Lucas' life, biological mother or not. Her pouncing on him, wanting to talk or whatever it is she wants to do, would disrupt our order, and send Lucas spinning. Yes,

I want him to know his mother, but only if she plans to stick around. No way will I let her forge a relationship if she plans to up and leave again. The courts might have something else to say, but until then, I make the rules here.

"What's the matter with him?" she asks and tries to see around me, but I block her. "Why is he so whiny, and Jesse, he needs a haircut. What is going on here?"

How fucking dare she come in here and question what's going on here. It takes all my strength to keep myself calm. "He's getting over chicken pox. We've been in the house for a week." She blinks up at me, her eyes narrowed. "Let's meet at the park, okay. I'll drop him off and meet you there in half an hour."

She stares at me like she wants to say more, then nods. "Maybe I'll go to the bar, say hello to everyone," she says, like she's testing me, toying with me, and I can't figure out why. Unless she knows about Olivia and me.

"Let's just meet at the park," I say and strive to keep the worry from my voice. I don't want her just springing herself on Olivia. "I won't be long. I'll grab us a couple coffees, okay?"

She nods. "Fine. I'll be there at our bench."

Our bench. I almost choke. It's been a long time since anything has been ours.

Once she's in her car, I hustle Lucas outside, and he buckles himself in. With my heart pounding in my ears, and my mind racing a million miles an hour, I back out of my driveway and head to my grandmother's.

The second I step from the car, her face drops. "What's wrong, Jesse?" she asks, her gaze flying to Lucas as he kicks his door open.

I usher Lucas inside, and once he's out of earshot, I scrub my chin and lower my voice. "It's Kylie. She's back."

Her cloudy blue eyes go wide. "Oh my. I didn't expect to

hear you say that." She folds her hands. "I suppose we had to expect that one day she would show up."

"I know. But no contact in a year and she shows up on my doorstep. I don't know what to do."

"What does she want?"

"I'm about to find out. She wants to talk." I take a deep breath, and tug on my hair. "No matter what, Lucas comes first. I have to think about what's best for him."

"Of course you do. You have to think about what's best for you too, Jesse. You count in all this too, and we only get one shot at this thing called living." She offers me a soft smile, and puts her palm on my face. "You've been happy these last couple weeks, alive again. I've seen it with my own eyes. Don't let anyone take that from you, okay? You deserve it."

I'm intelligent enough to realize she's talking about Olivia. Intelligent enough to realize she's right. I *have* been happy. I love my son more than life, but I've only been going through the motions. When I'm with Liv, it's like the world is a brighter place, the dull gray now vibrant and exciting.

"You have a lot to figure out," Grandma says, and smiles. "But you will."

I laugh. She might have more faith in me than I have in myself.

"I'll do my best." I check my watch. "I'll be back in a couple of hours, okay?"

"Take all the time you need. Lucas and I are just fine."

I give her a kiss on the cheek, my throat so tight it's almost impossible to swallow. "Okay, thanks."

Back in my car, I glance at my phone and consider calling Olivia to warn her. Then again, if Kylie is just here to talk and plans to take off again, no one really needs to know. I park, grab a couple of coffees, and head to the bench in the park—the bench that used to be ours.

She's on her phone when I reach her, and she smiles up at me when I block the sun.

"Mmm, that smells good," she says as I hand her a cup. She pats the bench before me, but I'm so antsy, I'm not sure I can sit still. "Please, Jesse," she says. I drop down next to her and she asks, "How have you been?"

"We've been good," I say. "Lucas is doing well. He starts kindergarten this year."

"Does he still...you know."

I frown at her. "Does he have high-functioning autism, you mean?" She nods, and I expel an exaggerated breath. "He'll always have it, Kylie. It's not something he's going to grow out of."

"Mom and Dad said you don't bring him around or call anymore."

"He had a bit of a hard time last time, and I got the sense they weren't interested in seeing him anymore."

"Yeah, they said he had a total fit."

Jesus.

"Yeah, something like that." I take a sip of my coffee. "Why are you here?"

"Way to get right to the point." She laughs and makes light of it, but the stone in my stomach weighs me down. I don't answer. "Okay, well, I thought maybe I'd come back and see how you were."

"Why now?"

"I just thought it was time."

"Are you staying?"

She shrugs, and moves her leg so it's touching mine. "Maybe."

"Kylie, if you think you can come here, and that I'm going to pick up where we were before you left, you're wrong."

She shrugs like she's not worried about that, like she can wrap me around her baby finger anytime she wants. I'm not sure she could ever do that with me, and so much has changed since our college years. I had to grow up fast when my parents died, and I was left with a young child to raise. I take that responsibility very seriously.

She sips her coffee and glances around. "I'd like to spend time with Lucas."

"I think Lucas should know his mother," I say, and she smiles at me. "But I can't let you into his life if you're going to disappear again. He has a hard time with change and disruptions to his schedule."

She arches one brow. "Does Olivia disrupt his schedule?"

At the mention of Liv, my pulse jumps. "Why do you ask that?"

"I saw her leaving your place."

Is that what this is all about? She doesn't like me spending time with Olivia? I almost laugh. What business is it of hers who I spend time with anyway?

"She helps me out, and I help her out."

A laugh bubbles in her throat. "Yeah, I just bet."

With my paper cup halfway to my lips, I stare at her over the lid. "What's that supposed to mean?"

"I heard there was more going on between you two."

"Listen, Kylie. Who I see is none of your business. It hasn't been for a long time. I'm not really sure why this would upset you."

"Who says it does?" I'm about to answer when she says, "I never meant to hurt you or Lucas. I just wasn't ready for all this, you know?"

I pinch the bridge of my nose. Is anyone ever really ready for all this? "Are you saying you are now?"

"I want to try."

"Hollywood didn't work out for you?" I shoot back, the trust we once shared shattered a long time ago. Trust is so damn important to me, and once it's been crushed...well, it's not something I can ever forgive, or easily get back.

She snorts. "What about you, Jesse? Still running the bar?" she asks, her lips twisted as she throws that back at me.

"Yeah, I am."

She nods. "So, you've just given up on your future, then?"

I fight down the burst of anger. Why is my future suddenly so important to everyone? "I didn't give up on anything. I've been taking care of our son, in case you haven't noticed."

"So that's it, then. You're just going to let your dreams die?"

"I'm not going to abandon anyone to pursue them," I say.

"Well, now that I'm back, maybe I can take care of Lucas while you go to med school."

She couldn't handle Lucas when he was a toddler, what makes her think she can handle him now? But I don't say that. Instead I ask, "Why are you really here?"

"Jesse," she says softly, changing tactics. "Can you please give me a second chance?"

"Kylie—"

"I made a mistake. A big one. I was young and stupid, and...dreams are important, you know."

"I know. I also know you resented us for keeping you from them."

"You told me to go."

"Of course, I did. I didn't want you here, hating everything about this life."

"I never said I hated it. It just wasn't what I signed on for."

"No, you signed on to be a doctor's wife, and I didn't live up to my side of the bargain. I get it, Kylie. I really do."

Tears fall down her face and because I'm not a total prick, I put my arm around her. There was a time I loved this woman, and I can't just push her out of my life now, not when she's the mother of our son.

"Tell me I can have another chance," she says.

I take a huge breath. "If you're here to stay, and you're serious, you can have another chance—" Before I can finish, and tell her she can have a chance with Lucas only, and that the visits would be short and supervised by me and he wouldn't be told she was his mother until she proved herself to us, she throws herself into my arms, and my coffee cup goes flying.

"Oh, Jesse, thank you. You won't be sorry."

My stomach cramps, because I think I already am. "Wait, I need to explain—"

"I have to go. My mother is waiting for me."

"Kylie, wait," I say but she's gone. I shake my head, and when a shadow blocks my path, I glance up.

"Cup of coffee?" Callan asks. "You look like you could use another cup or ten."

I shake my head. "That obvious, huh?"

He looks past my shoulders. "Ah, was that Kylie?"

"Yeah, she's back." He gives a low slow whistle. "What?" I ask.

"Just you're with her best friend now, and you know how girls can be?"

My stomach jumps. "Yeah, I do," I say. I have to talk to Olivia. Now. Not only to tell her Kylie is back asking for things I have no intention to give her, but to lay my heart on the line and see where we go from there.

"Although rumor has it you and Olivia aren't serious."

"Where did you hear that?"

"Colin." He looks around like he expects Colin to suddenly materialize and I hope he doesn't. I'm in such a shit mood, anything could set me off. I'm normally calm and even tempered, but right now, with the world closing in on me, and fearing it could go to hell, I might react with my fist before my brain.

"I think he likes her," he adds.

"Yeah, I know."

He glances over his shoulder, and I notice his daughter playing catch with Gemma.

"But as far as Olivia and I not being serious, don't believe everything you hear," I say, and he nods like he totally gets it.

He shoves his hands into his pockets. "I don't."

I push to my feet and eye him. "Are you and Gemma together?" I ask. He's not said anything to me at the bar, or at support group, but I know him well enough that I'm comfortable asking. I also know it's taken a lot for him to get his life in order after his wife was run over by a drunk driver shortly after their daughter was born. My heart hurts just thinking about it. Now if there was ever a guy who needed to move on and find love, it's him. He drags one hand from his pocket and grips his hair. The fact is, though, he loved his wife, and I'm not sure he can, or even wants to move on. For his daughter's sake, he goes from one day to the next, much like I do. He needs more.

I need more.

"It's complicated," he admits.

I put my hand on his shoulder. "Complicated I understand."

"Like really fucking complicated."

"I understand that, too."

He nods, looks at the ground for a second and when his eyes meet mine, there is a deep understanding there. "Yeah, I think you do."

"Come by for a beer this week." I give him a wink. "I'm a good listener."

"Sounds good, man." He jerks his thumb. "I should get back."

"Okay, see you. I need to get to the pub, anyway."

I hurry back to my car, anxious to see Olivia. We need to talk. We've needed to talk for a long time now and with Kylie back in the picture wanting to pick up where we left off, I need to know where Olivia stands. Yeah, it's complicated. I don't want her to go, but I can't ask her to stay. I don't know what is next for us, all I know is we need to get everything out in the open. Fuck, for all I know she still wants Colin.

If she did, would she have kissed you, or made love to you, the way she had?

I drive the short distance to work, and squeeze my vehicle in between two trucks. It's busy as it usually is on a Friday afternoon, and I hope Olivia isn't run off her feet. We need to talk. Inside, I glance around and spot Colin and a few of the other off-duty firefighters playing a game of pool. My gaze lands on Jack and Heidi watching the big screen. I catch Jack's glance and a worried look comes over his face.

Shit, what is going on?

"Tara have you seen Olivia?" I ask when she walks by, empty tray in hand.

"She's in the office." I'm about to walk away when she captures my arm. "Listen, Boss, about this breakup—"

"Not now, Tara. Olivia and I need to talk."

"Yeah, you do," she says, her face so serious my heart stalls.

"What?" I ask.

She opens her mouth, then shuts it. What is going on with her? "Nothing," she finally says. "Go."

I hurry to my office, and catch Olivia dumping the contents of her backpack on the desk. She roots through the contents and snatches up her lip balm. She's about to open it and her head lifts when she hears me enter.

"Oh, hey," she says. "I was looking for my lip balm and you're not going to believe this, but I can't find my key, and..."

Her words fall off as I stand there, every muscle in my body tense. "Wait, what's going on? Why are you here?"

My gaze drops, takes in the brochures on my desk. Blood pumps faster through my veins, and the room closes in on me. I drive my clenched hands into my pockets, and lift my gaze to the woman staring at me.

"Why would you do this, Olivia?"

17

OLIVIA

"Oh, it's just..." I begin, but my words fall off when his jaw clenches so hard, I'm sure he's going to break teeth. In all the years I've known Jesse, I don't think I've ever seen him so angry, not even when Kylie up and left him and Lucas. "Jesse?"

"What makes everyone think they know what's best for me, Olivia?" he asks through clenched teeth, the muscles in his jaw rippling.

His head lifts, and his blue eyes are arctic, instantly freezing the blood racing through my veins. Holy hell, I've never been the focus of such scrutiny before.

"I just thought—"

"Stop," he says and tugs on his hair so hard, I'm sure it's going to leave a bald patch. He walks up to the lockers, his broad back covered in a navy T-shirt, and pounds a fist against the metal cabinets. Not hard enough to dent them, or bruise himself, but definitely loud enough for the noise to be heard from the bar area. I almost run and shut the door, but my legs are frozen in place.

What the hell is going on with him?

Every muscle in his body is tight, so tight, I'm worried something is going to snap.

"Is Lucas okay?" I ask tentatively, trying to pry the problem out of him, and praying to God his son is okay.

"He's fine," he grumbles, his voice clipped, his eyes now blazing as he turns back to me. "Am I not good enough for you, Liv?" A sound crawls out of his throat. A humorless laugh, mixed with a snort, as he jerks his head toward the brochures. "Not good enough unless I go back to school?"

Why would he say that to me? Does he not realize I only want the best for him? That I'd walk the highest mountain, and swim the largest ocean to see this man fulfill his dreams and live a happily ever after? Of all people, all the sacrifices, he deserves that. Do I want to be a part of those dreams? Hell, yes I do, even if it means switching schools and trying in vitro, to give him the family that he wants.

But what if I can't give him the family he wants?

Would I be holding him back from fulfilling *all* his dreams?

And what about my father?

I don't know. I just don't know the answers to anything. I only know I love this man with every fiber of my being, and I can't take him not being in my life. But whatever is going on with him right now is scaring the crap out of me.

"Jesse..." I take a step toward him and reach for his arm, wanting to pull him to me and tell him no matter what it is, we can work through it together.

But can we?

He holds his hands up to stop me. "Don't." A fast shake of his head. "Maybe you're not so different after all."

My arm drops, and the energy emanating off him wraps around me and spreads dread and worry through my body. "Different from what...or maybe I should be asking who?" I query, but nausea wells up inside my tight stomach as he glares at me. I put my hand over my belly. I don't need him to answer that question. I'm pretty damn sure I already know. The hairs on the back of my neck stand on edge. The way they did when I was leaving his place earlier today.

Kylie.

I falter backward, until my legs hit his desk. She's back in town. That has to be the logical answer here. "Kylie," I murmur.

"Yeah."

His nostrils flare as he inhales, and he bends forward, places his hands on his knees and takes a few more breaths.

"What did she want?" I ask, not sure if I want to hear the answer as my gaze goes to the brochures. Jesse's head lifts, and his gaze follows mine.

Are these brochures a reminder of what he lost because he didn't follow his dream, choosing instead to follow his parents? Does this anger mean he still loves Kylie, that he wants her back in his life? I'm not sure, but to accuse me of being just like her...

I don't think so.

I picked up those brochures out of love. How could he think otherwise? My own anger coils tightly inside me, a snake preparing to strike, but I bite it back, desperate to get to the bottom of matters, because I have to be reading this situation wrong.

The alternative is too painful to consider.

"Is that what you think, Jesse?" I ask, fighting like hell to understand what's really going on here. Someone walks by the open office door, and I stiffen. Looks like all the staff are trying to figure out what the hell is going on between the two of us.

They're not the only ones.

He pushes to his full height, scoops the brochures from his desk and waves them. "You tell me." He tosses the papers back onto the desk and they scattered. "Actually, the fact that you picked these up says it all."

I'm so rattled, I can barely get my words out, but I'm not sure what to say. This man that I've known and have loved all of my life just put me in the same category as his ex, who up and left him and his child and never looked back. Tears pound behind my eyes and I desperately work to keep them from falling. He doesn't deserve my tears.

"I...uh..." I try to speak but my words get stuck in my throat. Then again, does he even deserve an explanation from me.

"Yeah, that's what I thought." He scoffs. "Ready to stage that breakup?" he asks, his face and eyes so hard, I'm not even sure I'm looking at my neighbor anymore. He might be standing before me, looking like the guy I know, but he's not acting anything like him.

My legs nearly go out from underneath me as he casts cold eyes my way. Is this really happening? It's all coming at me so fast I can't quite get my thoughts straight. But one thing rings loud and clear. We. Are. Done.

Maybe even our friendship.

Could this day get any worse? I swallow against the lump pushing into my throat. It was the one thing we were supposed to protect, and once this smoke clears, I'm not even sure we can put the pieces back together again—not after him accusing me of being just like his ex. After everything we shared, the openness and honesty between us...

Were you honest, Olivia?

Did you tell him how you really felt?

The obvious answers to those questions are a big fat no. Would things have been different had I opened up in the beginning and told him the truth? I guess I'll never know. Not now, anyway.

"I guess so," I say, working to keep my cool despite the tsunami in my stomach.

He stalks to the door, "We're done, Olivia." He waves a finger back and forth between the two of us. "It's been fun, but Kylie is back now," he says, his fingers gripping the doorknob so tight, it's a wonder it doesn't snap off.

"Yeah, it's been fun," I say, working to put effort into my words as I smooth my hair from my face. "I have to leave for California soon anyway."

He shakes his head, and I get it. I'm the second girl in his life to head to California for bigger and better. Maybe that wouldn't have happened if he hadn't come at me like I was a matador's cape and he was the frothing bull.

Now, everything is ruined, and irreparable.

"Yeah. Okay, so..." He pauses like he's searching for the right word, but instead of finding it, he turns and leaves. The room chills, every single bone in my body shaking, and I drop into the chair, my legs no longer able to keep me standing. Seconds turn to minutes and I hug myself and work to get myself together. How can I go out there and face everyone after what just happened? How much did they actually hear? At least the breakup was believable, even though it was supposed to be a mutual thing, where we parted amicably.

We did anything but.

I take a couple deep breaths, then reach for my backpack. I scoop up my belongings, never planning to step foot in the pub again. Through blurry eyes, my fingers land on the brochures, and I pick them up and toss them into the trash can.

"Hey," Tara says, poking her head in.

I shake my head fast. "I don't want to talk about it." She stands there for a moment, like she's debating on what to do. "I'm okay," I lie.

She takes a deep breath and lets it out slowly. "I'm sorry, Olivia."

I have no idea why her face is twisted in a guilty frown. She set this in motion, it was her idea, but Jesse and I agreed to it. This isn't on her, it's on me.

"You have nothing to be sorry about." I push up and stand on wobbly legs, doing my damn best to display a confidence that I don't feel.

"I...maybe this was all a bad idea," she says.

Bad ideas. I almost snort. My first instinct was right. Nothing good can come from one.

"I have no idea what you're talking about. From what I understand, Colin is interested, right? Is he out there? Maybe I should go make a move."

"Olivia," she says her voice so full of sadness and regret, it scores my heart. "You don't have to do this."

"Do what?" I ask, injecting a lightness into my voice that I don't feel.

"Act like there was nothing between you and Jesse when I know full well there was."

I laugh and it sounds almost hysterical. "Maybe you need glasses, Tara." I sit up a little bit straighter. "We were acting."

I believe the Oscar goes to me for this particular performance.

"Olivia—"

"I need to go," I say. "Have to get home and get dinner up for Dad."

"I'll drive you," she says and starts to untie her apron.

"No, I could use the fresh air." I say, and forcing one leg in front of the other, I step out into the sunshine. I lean against the building, and swipe the stupid tears from my eyes. A car pulls into the parking lot, and hoping it's someone I don't know I push off the wall. I'm about to bolt, when someone calls my name.

Oh, God. No!

Here I thought this day couldn't get any worse.

"Kylie," I say as she comes straight at me, each step fast and determined. I swallow and hope she can't tell I've been crying. "You're back."

She grins. "You always were a smart one."

The sarcasm in her voice catches me off guard. Okay, so maybe she's mad that I hadn't responded to her text.

"Welcome home," I say. "How—"

"Let's cut right to the chase here," she interjects. "I know you've been fucking around with Jesse."

"I...what?" Kylie wobbles in front of me as my vision goes a little fuzzy. I guess Brit must have told her after all. "Kylie, you were gone."

She plants one hand on her hip and glares at me. "Now I'm back and Jesse and I are going to try to work things out."

My heart jumps into my throat. "Did he...say that?"

She cocks her head and eyes me, like I have the nerve to ask the question. "Yes, he said that. Why would you have such a hard time believing that?"

Because I thought he'd moved on.

With me.

I thought wrong.

"No reason. I believe it," I say, and make a move to go, but she puts her hand on my arm to stop me.

"Did you really think you could just take my place?"

"I...wasn't trying to. No one heard from you for a year, Kylie."

"So, you thought you'd just hone in." She shakes her head in disgust. "My God, you are so pathetic."

"What the hell?" Why is she talking to me like this? Where is this anger coming from? I've always been a good friend to her. Right up until she dropped Jesse and Lucas from her life for good last year.

She shakes her head, like I'm an idiot. "He was using you, Olivia. Scratching an itch until I returned."

"It wasn't like that," I say. Or was it? He's never been attracted to me in all these years. Was he only just satisfying a need? Was I so wrong to think there could have been more between us?

She rolls her eyes and laughs. "You and your stupid crush."

"Wait, what?"

"Oh, come on. You've had it bad for him since I first met you."

I blink once, then twice hardly able to believe what I'm hearing. "You knew that?"

"Everyone knew that."

"If you knew that, why did you go after him?"

She laughs. "You mean like girl code. You're one to talk."

"You've been gone a long time, Kylie," I say in my defense. I never would have been intimate with Jesse if I thought they stood a chance. Heck, I'm the one that told her to go for it.

"Like you ever had a real chance with him," she says. "Look at you and look at me."

I fold my arms and hug myself, feeling like that young girl in seventh grade when the mean girls zeroed in on me. "Why are you doing this, Kylie?"

"I'm tired of you being the fucking golden child, getting everything you've ever wanted."

"When have I ever gotten anything I wanted?"

"Your father doted on you," she spits out, her eyes full of jealousy and resentment. "Jesse's mother treated you like a daughter. Jesse would walk through fire for you. You had everything I ever wanted."

"Are you kidding me?" I blurt out. "You had everything, Kylie." Or at least I thought she did.

"My mother and step-dad bought me things, their way of

showing love, but you had the real deal, Olivia. I took Jesse from you then, and I'm taking him back now."

The chaos in my mind settles, and my heart stops beating as understanding dawns. All the anger, hate and disappointment she had in her life, she directed at me. Then and now.

"This is about me," I say, my heart hurting, for her, Jesse, Lucas, for all the hate and love and loss.

She laughs. "It's always been about you."

A fresh wave of tears sting my eyes and my throat is so tight it's hard to get my words out. "Did you ever even love Jesse?"

She rolls one shoulder. "Yeah, of course."

Spoken like a woman who has no idea what love is.

"There are a couple of things you should know. My life wasn't perfect, contrary to what you might think. You might have had to move because your mother remarried, but your real father was still in your life. I *lost* a mother, and I *lost* Jesse's parents—who were like parents to me." She rolls her eyes, but I grab her arm and tug. She's about to complain, but I cut her off and say, "And I was never jealous of what you had, Kylie. I was always happy for you and wanted what was best, which is why I encouraged you to go for Jesse. I was wrong, though. You're not what's best for Jesse. I am."

She laughs, but I don't miss the worry behind it. "Well, too late for that."

The pub door opens, and out walks Colin. He takes one look at me, and worry crosses his face.

"Olivia, are you okay?"

"Stay away from us," Kylie says and walks away.

I'm about to sag against the wall when Colin tugs me to him. "You're not okay. I'm taking you home," he says, and everything else that happens after that, from him putting me in his car, driving me down the road, and helping me from the passenger seat, to seeing Jesse watching us from his driveway, runs through my mind like a blur, like I'm watching someone else's life crumble around them.

Colin helps me inside, and I'm glad Dad is home because once again, my stupid key is gone. Dad pales when he sees me.

"Olivia?"

"I need to pack. I'm going to California to find us a place to live."

18

JESSE

It's been almost a week since I acted like a complete dick in my office. A week since I'd last seen Olivia. From what her father told me, she hopped on a plane and went to California to find them a place to live. I don't blame her for leaving. I was a total jerk, but when I saw those brochures, something inside me snapped and I completely lost my cool.

I spent the last fucking week thinking about everything I'd said to her, everything she *didn't* say to me, because I wouldn't give her a chance. I accused her of being like Kylie, which was a pretty shitty thing to do. She's nothing like my ex, and deep down I'm sure she's just pushing for me to go back to school because she cares about me.

So why did you lose your cool, dude?

Oh, maybe on some level I was pushing her away before she could leave me—us. Dr. Phil would have a field day with that one, but after so much loss, I think I was terrified of Olivia leaving us, even though I wouldn't want to do anything to keep her from her dreams.

I am so fucked up.

The look on her face still haunts me and I said the one thing we had to protect was our friendship. I did a pretty shitty job of that. I'm sure she'll never speak to me again, and I don't blame her one bit.

Tara told me Kylie showed up outside the pub after I stormed out, but she has no idea what transpired between the two. All she said was that Colin was there to pick up the pieces—after I shattered her with my accusations.

A sound catches in my throat. I guess in the end, it's all for the best. She ended up with the guy she wanted, and is headed out west to the school of her dreams. Lucas and I will move forward—somehow—like we always do. I glance at the brochures in front of me. I fished them out of my garbage can before dumping it. I'm not sure why, but now here I am, staring at a picture of Harvard medical school and trying to figure out what's next.

"Daddy, you're growling. Are you a T-Rex?" Lucas asks, as I sit on the back deck with him, staring off into space and kicking my own ass as he plays with his toys.

"Yeah, buddy, I'm a T-Rex," I say and hold my hands up, making claws with my fingers.

The doorbell rings and my heart leaps. I jump from my chair, hoping it's Olivia. Then I remember Kylie was coming over. She's been here to see Lucas a few times this week. He hasn't paid her much attention, and her patience with him is running thin. She promised she was home for good, which is the only reason I'm letting her get to know him—under my supervision. Yet there is a part of me that doesn't believe her.

"Your mother is here," I say to Lucas.

"Daddy, why isn't Olivia my mother?"

I shake my head. Leave it to my son to ask the question of all questions. I crouch beside him.

"Because Kylie is your mom. You like her, don't you?"

He shrugs and my heart squeezes. "I don't think she likes my dinosaurs."

"Why do you say that?"

"She never wants to play with them."

"Give her some time, okay," I say, and hate that I'm asking that of him. She's the one who should be trying, not the other way around.

"I like Olivia. She plays with my dinosaurs," he says. "When are we going to Madelyn's birthday party?"

"A little later today," I say. I have to drop Lucas off and get to the office to take care of some paperwork. I step into the house, and open the door for Kylie. Dressed in short denim cutoffs and a tight T-shirt, she beams up at me.

"Hey," she says, her voice light and flirty. Her antics might have worked on me once, but I've grown up a lot since then. I had to.

"Come on in." I step away and wave her in. "Lucas is out back."

She touches my arm. "I thought we could talk first."

I exhale, already knowing where she's going with this. Two days ago, when she was here, she pressed to get back together, I set her straight, but she clearly won't take no for an answer. Gut instinct tells me she's lost and I'm the easiest solution. Of course, she's also pressing me to go back to school. Isn't everyone. But for different reasons. I came to that conclusion once I was able to think with clarity.

"Kylie, I'm letting you into Lucas' life, not mine."

"Aren't you two a package deal?"

Ignoring that, I pinch the bridge of my nose and make my way through the house. She follows behind and we step out onto the back patio.

"We have to leave in an hour," I tell her. "Lucas has a birthday party."

"Hi Lucas."

"Hi," he says, his focus on something else entirely.

"You should look at your mother when you're speaking to her," she says, her voice lacking empathy or patience for her son.

Lucas continues to play with his dinosaurs, but I don't miss the stiffening of his body.

"Kylie," I say quietly. "You know he has trouble in social situations. Give him time to get used to you."

"How is he going to learn if you never correct him?"

"It's not quite like that."

She arches her brow like she doesn't quite believe that. "Mom and Wallace want to see him."

"I don't want to go, Daddy," Lucas bursts out.

Kylie opens her mouth, and I put my hand up. "Let's just enjoy this afternoon, okay? We can talk about a visit later."

She sits at the table, and I go inside to get us all lemonade. When I come back out, Kylie straightens, and has an almost guilty look on her face. She'd obviously been talking to Lucas about something that's agitating him, judging by the way he's pulling on the neck of his t-shirt.

"Lucas, do you want to play a game?"

He sits up. "Dinosaurs and ladders?"

"Sure, go grab it."

He leaps to his feet and heads inside.

"I don't really like board games," Kylie says and takes a sip of her lemonade.

I frown at her. Does she even want to be here? "What would you prefer to do?"

"I think we need to talk, Jesse. About us."

"Okay, fine. There is no us, and now that you're home to stay, what do you plan to do with your life?"

She frowns. "I haven't given it much thought. My stepfather said he could give me a job, but as a receptionist for a real estate firm. No thank you."

"What exactly is it you want to do, then?"

"I wanted to be your wife."

"You wanted to be a doctor's wife."

She curls her finger in her hair, not denying that.

"Do you even want to be back here?" I ask.

"I *had* to come back."

"Had to?"

"Once I heard about you and Olivia, I—"

"That's why you're back? You were worried about Olivia and me hooking up?"

Instead of answering, she says, "What the hell did she think she was doing anyway?" She rolls her eyes. "Ah, girl code, and she's so not your type, Jesse. It made me wonder what was going on with you."

First, Olivia *is* my type, and what goes on with me is none of her business.

"Did you really just expect me to sit here and wait for you?"

"Well you have been, haven't you? I mean, you haven't been with anyone."

Wow, just wow. What did I ever see in this woman?

"I've been busy taking care of our son, and running a business, Kylie."

I stop talking when Lucas comes running out with his game. I help him set it up on the table and for the next half hour, we play. Kylie grows bored rather quickly, and checks her watch a few times.

"Somewhere to be?" I ask her.

"It's fine." She crinkles her nose. "It's just this audition..."

"Audition. Here in Boston?"

"Well, not exactly."

"So, you're going back then?" I shake my head. Why the hell did I ever believe her, or let her into Lucas' life again?

She's just here to lay claim to something that isn't hers. Not anymore, anyway.

I check my watch. "I actually need to go pack his bag for the party. Are you two okay out here alone while I run inside?"

"Of course we are," Kylie says.

"Daddy, I want to go to the party."

"We are, kiddo. I'm going to go get your things."

I leave the two of them alone, reluctantly, and dash upstairs to Lucas' bedroom. I pack his bag with a few of his favorite toys, and I'm about to toss in his headphones when his wail reaches my ears. I rush to the window and glance out. What the hell is going on?

He's holding something in his hand and bent over, and Kylie is trying to pry it from his fingers.

"Let it go, Lucas. It's not your turn. You need to learn the rules. You can't get away with things just because you're different. You're babied too much."

I stand there dumbfounded. Did she really just call my son a name and berate me for my parenting skills all in one breath? This woman has no idea how to take care of her son.

Lucas screams louder, and before I can drop everything and get downstairs, Olivia is there, allowing me to breathe again. Sweet Olivia, the sweet girl from next door, reaches for Lucas and cradles him in her arms. He calms from her touch and soothing words.

"What are you doing here?" Kylie says. "I told you to stay away from us. Jesse and I are working things out."

She told her to stay away?

She told her we were working things out?

"What about you and Lucas? Are you trying to work things out with him too?" Olivia shoots back. "If you are, you're doing a bad job of it."

I swallow. Olivia is mild-mannered, but when push comes

to shove, she'll protect those she cares about, and she cares about my son.

She cares about me, too.

Why did I have to fuck everything up?

"Not that it's any of your business, but he won't listen to me," Kylie says.

Olivia puts her hands over Lucas' ears to reduce the stimuli. "Then stop screaming at him."

"I am not screaming," she yells.

Olivia gives an exasperated sigh. "Please calm yourself down. For your son's sake."

"I've had enough of this." She stands up, and runs her hand down her hair. "That child is out of control. I think the courts need to be involved here."

I drop everything, and hurry down the stairs.

"No, Kylie. You're out of control." My glance goes from Kylie to Olivia and I give her a grateful smile.

"You've got to be kidding me!" Kylie says.

I eye her. "About what?"

"You like...her?" she jerks her finger toward Olivia. "Desperate much?"

Anger hits sure and swift, and my fingers curl. She can say whatever she wants to me, but I won't stand for her hurting my son, or the woman I love. My gaze flies to Olivia, and her eyes are cast downward, but I know the dig—from her former best friend—had to sting.

"I think it's time for you to leave."

"Fine, you'll be hearing from my lawyer."

"Go ahead, get the courts involved. Let's see how favorable that will be for you."

"I..." She hesitates for a moment. She won't get the courts involved because that might end up with her having responsibility in raising our son. "I don't need any of this."

"We weren't asking any of this from you, Kylie," I say. "We were doing just fine."

She shakes her head and huffs off, and I get the feeling that we won't be seeing much of her anymore. I just wish I'd been smarter and not let her into Lucas' life until she proved herself worthy.

I wish I'd been smarter with Olivia too.

I glance at the woman I love as she releases Lucas from the circle of her arms. I take a step toward them. We need to talk, but I'm not certain she agrees.

"Olivia..."

She puts her hand on Lucas' shoulder and squeezes. "See you later, Lucas." She steps off the deck. I stare at her as she cuts through the backyard and enters her own—taking a big part of me with her.

I want to make this right between us again. I *need* to make it right. I might want more from her, in my life and in my bed, but if I can't have that, I at least want her friendship.

What do I have to do to fix this between us?

19

___

OLIVIA

___

For the last week and a half, since my fight with Jesse, I've been walking around numb, doing everything I can to fight off the tears. He seemed like he wanted to talk the other day, but what do we have left to say to each other? Maybe this is the way things were supposed to work out.

When I walked out of the bar that day, it was with the intention of never stepping foot in it again, and I don't plan to. I'm still having a hard time wrapping my brain around Kylie, and how vile she was to me. I've never been anything but nice to her, but underneath her polished exterior, I guess her true colors finally showed.

I'm sad that she can't be the mother Lucas needs, and that she disrupted his life once again, before bailing and heading back to California. I'll be bailing and heading there myself soon enough. A huge lump forms in my throat. When it comes right down to it, it's not what I want at all.

I'm waiting on the realtor, wanting to talk to her about putting the house up for sale, when my cell phone rings. I tug it from my pocket and my pulse leaps when caller ID informs me it's Dad. He's at paint night with Heidi. I hope everything is okay.

"Hey Dad," I say. "What's up?"

"Can you come to the pub?"

My first reaction is no...hell no, but there's something in his voice that gives me pause.

"Are you okay?"

"No," he says flatly.

With panic erupting inside me, I say, "I'll be right there." I dash outside, the sun setting low on the horizon as I try to run to the pub, all my parts jiggling. But I'm not too worried about that. No one is looking at me, and I don't hate those parts anymore, thanks to Jesse.

Jesse.

The guy next door I've been crazy about since...forever. The guy who awakened me in the bedroom, the guy who worshipped my body, and taught me to love myself.

The guy who accused me of something awful.

My heart is pounding out of my chest by the time I reach the pub. I push open the heavy door, and glance around but can't find my father anywhere. I spot Tara and run to her.

"Tara, where is Dad? He called and said he wasn't okay."

"Come with me," she says, and takes my arm. She guides me to the back, to Jesse's office and I hesitate.

"What's going on?"

"Your father is in the office. We all need to talk."

She ushers me in and Dad is standing there, a strange look on his face. My gaze goes from him, to the dozen or more keys—my keys—sprawled across Jesse's desk. The same desk he bent me over and rocked my world.

"What...what is this?"

"I have a confession," he says.

"Me too," Tara pipes in.

"Why...what? My keys?"

"I've been sneaking them out of your bag," Dad says. "Tara has been too." I glance at Tara, who has a sheepish look on her face.

"Why?" I ask.

Dad clears his throat. "So you couldn't get in the house."

I shake my head, stupefied. "Why didn't you want me to get in the house?"

"If you couldn't get in, you'd be forced to go to Jesse's," Dad says.

What is he talking about? "I have no idea what is going on here."

"Have a seat," Tara says and walks me around the desk. I drop down into Jesse seat, and glance at my Dad and Tara, never having felt so weary in my life. Dad sits on the desk beside me, and Tara moves toward the lockers.

"This is all our fault," Tara says.

"I don't get it."

"Well," she begins and exchanges a look with Dad. "We all know you like Jesse. Like really, really like him. Always have." I open my mouth but she holds her hand up to cut me off. "Just hear me out, please."

"Okay."

"Your dad wants all your decisions to be yours. He'd never tell you he didn't want to move."

"Dad?" I sit up a little straighter. "You don't want to move?"

"Let me finish, Olivia," Tara says.

I swallow and sink back into the chair. Where is she going with this?

"We kind of set you up. You know, just to open your eyes. You thought you were opening Colin's eyes, but in actuality, we were opening yours. At least we were trying to."

"Okay, slow down," I say as I try to piece this together. "Opening my eyes?"

"I know it wasn't Colin you were into. He was in on this, too. Pretending to like you, flirt with you and things like that to make Jesse jealous. It worked."

"You guys were meddling in my life?" I glare at my father. "Dad, come on. Seriously?"

"We just think you and Jesse belong together, is all," Tara explains. "We wanted to put you guys in a situation where you could both see how right you were for each other."

My stomach tightens, and I glance at the garbage can, sure I'm going to throw up.

"Does Jesse know this?"

Tara scrunches up her face. "Yeah. I'm lucky to still have a job."

I rake my hand through my hair. "He must be furious." I know I am.

"You could say that," Tara says.

Dad reaches out and takes my hand. "You two kids need to talk."

I don't want to talk to him. "Dad, do you not want to move?"

"You're a smart girl. You make good choices. You'll know what to do when the time comes." He squeezes my hand in reassurance. "I'll stand behind whatever it is you want to do."

"But Dad, I'm not going to—"

"Olivia," he says, his fatherly voice firm. "Talk to Jesse. He's hurting, too."

As soon as the words leave his mouth, Jesse comes into the office. His feet skid to an abrupt halt when he finds the three of us inside. Dad and Tara make a beeline for the door. In the hall, Dad grabs hold of the knob.

"We're not letting you out, until you two talk."

I jump from my chair. "Dad, you can't—"

The door slams shut on my protest, and I groan.

Jesse stares at me and I begin to pick up the keys. "Can you believe those two?" I say.

"Three, Colin was in on it too."

"I'm sorry, Jesse. I'm sure this is all Dad's doing, and I'm sorry you got dragged into it."

"I'm sorry, too."

His words sting a bit, and my hands shake a little as I gather up the keys. I thought there was more to us, that we might have had a chance. But if he's sorry, I must have read everything wrong.

"But I'm not sorry they tricked us into a pretend relationship."

My gaze jerks to his. "No?" I ask, and that's when I notice the fine lines around his eyes. Has he been getting any sleep? I know I've been lying awake at night for over a week now.

"No, I'm an asshole, and what I'm sorry for is the cruel things I said to you." He swallows and takes a measured step toward me. He stops and waits to see how I'm going to react. When I fall back into my chair, he says. "I'm also sorry for the way Kylie treated you. She's not—"

"She's not my friend."

There's a deep sadness in his eyes. "No, she's not. She's not anyone's friend."

"I'm not sure what I ever did to her."

"You didn't do anything to her. This is all her, not you. She's angry and confused, and lost. I want her to find herself, and happiness, but she's not going to find it here, or with us. You've been a good friend, Olivia. To her and to me."

I nod, but wonder if we can ever be friends again. Actually, I don't want that, anyway.

"You're nothing like Kylie. I was angry with her for just showing up like that, and she was pushing my buttons before I came here to talk to you. When I saw the brochures, I—"

"Reacted," I say, and as my anger melts away, it leaves

room for common sense to move in. He's had loss, and has been hurt, so he was pushing me away before I could leave him. Why didn't I realize that before? The brochures triggered something in him, but that also means he wanted more with me, but was worried I needed more from him, that he wasn't good enough just the way he is.

"You see," he says and circles the desk. "I know you care about me. I know you picked up the brochures to give me a nudge, to fulfill my dreams, not because I wasn't good enough for you."

"Jesse, you're the best guy I know."

He angles his head, his face full of regret. "Even after I was shitty."

"Yes," I take a deep breath and let it out slowly. "Even after that."

He pulls something from the top drawer of his desk and drops it in front of me. "I did a thing."

"What's this?" I ask as I look at the manila folder.

"I'm going back to school, Liv."

My heart skips a beat as I lift my eyes to his. "You are?"

"Yeah."

Tears pool in my eyes. "Don't do it for me, Jesse. I love you just the way you are."

"You love me?"

An almost hysterical laugh bubbles in my throat. "Apparently, everyone knows that. Haven't you heard?"

"I love you too, Olivia."

My heart swells inside my chest, and it's a good thing I'm sitting or I'd fall.

Jesse loves me...

"I'm going back to school for me and for Lucas." He looks down for a second. "I'm going to sell the bar. It's time."

I nod, my voice stuck in my throat.

"Here's the thing. Selling and going back to school will be

the hardest thing I've ever done, but it's something I have to do. I realize that, now. It would be much better if you were in our lives, and I want to ask you to stay, but I can't, Liv." He tugs on his hair, looking lost and broken, and so damn frightened, my heart squeezes tight. "I can't ask you to give up on your dreams and grow to resent us. But know this. I want you to stay, but I also understand you need to go. No matter what, I want us to be together." Dark lashes blink over hopeful eyes. "Maybe we can make the long-distance work."

"No."

He nods, and the muscles in his throat tighten. A moment of silence and then he says, "I understand." He takes a shaky breath. "Can we at least go back to being friends?"

"I don't want to be friends."

He grips the edge of the desk, his knuckles turning white. "Man, I really fucked this up."

"Yeah, you did. You're kind of a dumbass."

His gaze flies to me. "What?"

I grin at him. "You *fucked* me up, and I loved every second of it. You taught me so much about myself, Jesse, and opened my eyes, not just to what I wanted, but to what I needed. You gave me courage, enough courage to tell you how I really feel about you. I should have done it a long time ago, but I was afraid of losing you."

"I was afraid of losing you, too," he says. "But you just said you don't want to be friends."

"I don't." I stand, and put my hands on his cheeks. "I want to be more, and no, we can't make long distance work, because I'm not going anywhere."

The emotions that cross his eyes nearly floor me: love, hope, happiness...and fear. "Olivia, but your dreams. I can't..."

"I can go to school here, Jesse. Dad doesn't want to move, and honestly, neither do I. You and Lucas, you're the family I always wanted but never thought I could have." A sound catches in his throat as he cups my cheeks, his lips finding mine for a kiss steeped in love, passion and promise. When he breaks it, I add, "It's your dreams I'm worried about."

He frowns, his gaze moving over my face in deep confusion. "I don't understand. I'm going back to school."

"I'm talking about expanding your family. I might not be able to give you children, Jesse. I don't want you to grow to resent me. That's a big part of what's been holding me back."

He holds me tighter. "You and Lucas, you're all I need, Liv. If we have kids, we have kids, if we don't we don't."

"Are you sure?"

"I've never been more sure in my entire life. You're the world to me."

He picks me up off the ground and spins me around and a laugh bubbles out of my throat. When he sets me down, I grin at him.

"Do you hear that?" I ask.

He seems a bit embarrassed when he asks, "You mean my heart pounding?"

I laugh. "No, the murmurs outside the door." He glances at the door, and then turns those gorgeous blue eyes back on me.

"Should we make them sweat it out?" he asks.

"Hell yeah, we should. After all their interfering," I say.

"We'll have to thank them for that, huh?"

"Yeah, we will," I say with a chuckle. "But for now, they wait, and I think I know how we can pass the time. It might involve us sweating it out, too."

He steps up to the door and sets the lock. His smile is sexy and full of heat and mischief. "They think they're keeping us in, but it's us keeping them out."

"Us, I like the sound of that."

"You know what I like the sound of better?" He grips my t-shirt, toys with the hem.

"What?"

He lightly brushes his lips over mine. "Mr. and Mrs. Ward." He shrugs. "Or Mr. Ward and Ms. Bennett. However you want to do it."

My breath catches. Is he saying what I think he's saying? "Jesse?"

"Before I strip you naked—because I'm pretty sure when you tell this story to our grandkids, you don't want to be naked in it—I have a question to ask."

"Yes," I croak out.

"I love you, Liv. I have always loved you. You are the kindest and kinkiest—"

"Jesse," I say with a laugh and whack him.

He laughs with me. "I mean kindest, sweet, most beautiful woman I've ever set eyes on and I want to spend the rest of my life with you in it. Will you marry me? Will you be my wife, and Lucas' mother?"

I laugh, my heart so full of love and light, I just might float away.

"Yes, I will marry you. There is nothing I want more than to be your wife and Lucas' mother. Now hurry up and get your clothes off."

A knock comes on the door and I bite my lip playfully. "Seems like they're getting antsy out there. Is having sex here on your desk, with them all waiting for a verdict, a bad idea?"

"Hell yeah, it is," he says, and rips off his shirt.

My lighthearted laugh fills the room. "Bad ideas. Don't you just love them?"

***

Thank you so much for reading, **Single Dad on Tap**, I hope you loved this story as much as I loved writing it.Keep reading for an excerpt of **Single Dad Burning Up.**

. . .

Single Dad Burning Up

Callan:

"Daddy, I'm going to miss Chester."

I glance at my daughter, her mess of blonde hair bouncing as she skips down the near empty hallway beside me. Her bright sequined backpack is weighed down with a year's worth of artwork and the Chester she's referring to is the class pet, a cute guinea pig with white and butterscotch fur. With summer vacation now upon us—Kaitlyn's last day of kindergarten behind her—Chester will be going home with the teacher until the school years starts back up in the fall.

"I'm sure he's going to miss you too," I say, and ruffle her hair as the last of the kids rush from the school to enjoy their summer vacation. Luckily, I have the next few days off from the fire station and I was able to pick Kaitlyn up myself.

She pouts up at me, and my heart squeezes in my too-tight chest. She's been without a mother and baby brother for two years now, and every fucking morning, right after I peel my eyes open, I pray to God I can do right by her.

"Can we get a guinea pig?" she asks.

I swallow against the rawness in my tight throat, and grin at my little girl. I have such a hard time saying no to her, especially when she blinks up at me with those big blue eyes —her late mother's eyes.

"Please, Daddy."

I scrub my face, and remember the goldfish fiasco. Who knew overfeeding a goldfish would create ammonia in the bowl? I'm a firefighter, not a damn fish keeper. But, yeah, I should have Googled it. Kaitlyn shed a lot of tears in the makeshift funeral in our backyard, and I'd hate for her to go through that again. Then again, every child should have a pet, right? A guinea pig would be less work than a dog.

"We'll see, okay?" I say.

"Yay," she squeals and claps her hands. I can't help but smile. At six years old, she's smart enough to know 'we'll see' really means yes. My little girl has me wrapped around her pinky finger. I'm just glad I found the nail polish remover last night, after she painted said finger neon pink. The guys at the station would have gotten a kick out of that. They're all good guys though, even if they love to goad me. There isn't a single colleague that wouldn't jump to lend a helping hand, and she gets lots of motherly attention from her aunt Melissa—my late wife Zoe's younger sister—and both sets of grandparents, who dote on her.

I arch one brow. "You promise you'll take care of him?"

She gives me an enthusiastic nod, and I just shake my head as we round the corner. "I'm going to call him Gilbert."

"Why Gilbert?" I ask.

Her mouth drops open, like I might be dense. She's probably right. Just when I think I'm nailing this single parenting thing, she grows and changes, presenting different challenges and a hundred more Google searches. Can't wait for her teen years—said no dad ever.

"Because it's cute," she says.

I laugh, but it dies an abrupt death when I take the hallway corner and smack straight into something...or rather someone. A squeal of surprise wraps around me as books and papers and pens scatter to the floor at my feet. I reach out to steady the woman I nearly knocked on her ass.

"Whoa, are you okay?" I ask, instantly realizing I'd plowed right into Gemma Davis, an old friend from high school. She teaches seventh grade, so we rarely cross paths in the school, but I've always liked her. Zoe took Gemma under her wing when Gemma moved here in high school.

"I'm okay," Gemma says and lifts her head. A wide smile splits her lips when she sees it's me. "Callan. Hi. It's so good to see you, or rather, bump into you."

I sink down and begin to gather up her books. "Sorry, I wasn't paying attention."

Her gaze goes from me to my daughter. "How are you, Kaitlyn?" she asks as she crouches with me to clean up the mess.

"I'm getting a guinea pig," Kaitlyn sings out.

I groan, and cut Gemma a glance. "Lucky me, huh?"

Gemma grins at me. "Don't worry. You're not alone. I think every child in Mrs. Anderson's class wants a guinea pig now. Chester *is* awfully cute." She gives a roll of her shoulder. "I guess it could be worse. The class pet could have been a snake."

I eye her. "Don't tell me—"

"Not me," she says with a quick shake of her head that loosens a tendril of honey-blonde hair from the small clip straining to hold it all together. "Mr. Baily has one." She holds her hands up palms out. "Just preparing you for first grade."

I exhale, my shoulders slumping. "Maybe I shouldn't have given in so easily to the guinea pig." She chuckles as we finish gathering up her music sheets. "I hope I didn't mess everything up."

"It's fine," she says. "I've always wanted to hear Beethoven played out of order."

I cringe. "I'm—"

She puts her hand on my arm. "I'm kidding," she says, and when she realizes she has her hand on me, she pulls it back and clutches the papers tighter. "It's not a big deal. I have lots of time to get them in order, before my summer lessons start."

I swallow and work to ignore the sensations trickling through me. Christ, she barely touched me; it shouldn't be triggering any kind of reaction, especially around the vicinity of my crotch. Jesus, I haven't been with a woman since Zoe, and have no desire to be with anyone. I might not have seen Gemma in a while, but we go way back. No way should a simple touch from her spark something deep inside me. Awaken something that has lain dormant for a very long time now.

"Sounds like an exciting weekend," I tease. But who am I to talk? I can't remember the last time I've been to Burgers and Brews Pub with the guys. Maybe that's why my traitorous cock jumped to the occasion. The guys at the station are always trying to set me up—especially my best friend Mason and his wife Lisa. When Zoe was alive, we always hung out as couples, and our children played. Maybe I ought to take them up on it. Any girl I hook up with would have to know up front that a quick roll in the hay is all I'm looking for, though. I have no more to give.

"I'd prefer a weekend with my music sheets to your dangerous job any day, Callan," she says, her eyes wide. "Running into burning buildings." A quake goes through her. "No thank you."

"It's not so bad," I say and turn to look at Kaitlyn. She's spinning in circles, her arms wide, as she chants *Gilbert* over and over. For a child who's been through a lot, she's always happy and that brings a smile to my face. I must be doing something right. I turn back to Gemma, find her staring at me. The last time we talked she'd just taken the job at the school and was dating a police officer. I remember him being quite a bit older than her.

"How've you been?" I ask. "Are you still with...Ah..." Shit what was his name?

"Brad. No, we broke up. A few months ago."

She averts her gaze, her lids fluttering rapidly as her body tenses. Okay, I'm not an expert on reading body language or anything, but I've clearly hit a sore spot here. Did the guy break her heart or something?

"Oh, someone new?" I ask.

"Nope. No desire. I've decided single is the way to go." I frown at that—but who am I to talk? She plasters on a big smile and turns back to me. "But I'm great. Two months off school to bask in the summer sun. Though I will be helping out at the Boys and Girls club, and a few nights a week, I'll be giving private piano lessons."

"I want to play piano, Daddy," Kaitlyn says. "Can Miss Davis teach me?"

It's not the first time she's asked. Her mom played and always filled our house with music. "We'll—" I stop myself before spouting out my favorite response and getting Kaitlyn's hopes up. I don't even know if Gemma has room in her schedule. "How about we talk about it later?" I say.

Gemma gives me a wink, like she's fully aware of my dilemma with my daughter, and my inability to say no. "She almost had you there, didn't she?"

I chuckle. "I've got to get better at saying no."

"You're doing a fine job with her." She casts a look Kaitlyn's way, a look of longing in her eyes as a small smile touches her naked lips. For a second I wonder if her break-up with Brad had something to do with wanting kids. Obviously, she longs to be a mother. "She's a sweet little girl. Very kind and sincere. Like you."

"Shh," I say and glance around. "I've got a reputation to protect here."

Her lips quirk at the corner, then her smile falls. "You good, Callan?" she asks, her voice soft, and I get what she's asking, what people are still asking two years later.

"I'm good," I lie. I'm as good as can be expected, I guess. Truthfully is anyone ever 'good' again after losing their wife and unborn baby boy? I was once told that when you lose someone you have bad days and days that aren't as bad. I hate that I fully understand that now.

"Do you keep in contact with any of the old gang? Are you and Mason still friends? Wait, he's a firefighter too, right?"

"Yup, still best friends," I say. "Come on, I'll walk you out."

"Sure."

We head toward the doors, and the warm afternoon sun shines down on us, but it does little to loosen the tightness in my lungs. On those bad days, I walk around with an invisible band around my chest, squeezing tight. Who am I kidding? On those days that aren't as bad, the belt is still there. I'm not sure it will ever slacken, and maybe I don't want it to. Maybe I deserve the grief.

Gemma leans into me, her warmth and citrusy scent stirring the controlled storm in my body. Her voice is low, for my ears only when she whispers, "If she's serious about lessons, I do have an opening."

I nod, and consider it. "She would probably love it. Her mom..." I let my words fall off.

"I know," Gemma says, and glances at her feet. "We can talk about it more later if you want."

Her reaction isn't unusual. Most people avoid the subject of my wife. They don't know whether it will upset me or not. I'm glad they don't know how to react. It means they've not had loss.

"We can talk about it over ice cream," I say to Gemma.

"Ice cream," Kaitlyn belts out, and we both laugh.

"Nothing gets by her." I shake my head. "Unless you have other plans," I say, hoping she doesn't.

"I do," she says. A ridiculous sense of disappointment sits heavy in my gut and I work to ignore it. "But," she says brightly, holding up an index finger. "Ice cream first." A smile reaches her dark eyes when they meet mine. "It's been too long, Callan," she says in a soft voice. "Let's get caught up."

"I'd love that."

"Yay," Kaitlyn says, her hand sliding into mine. "Swing me, Daddy."

I pick her up under the arms, and give her a swing, and she squeals in delight. I set her down and she grabs my hand and Gemma's. "Now both swing me."

"Kaitlyn—" I begin, wanting to set boundaries when it comes to other people.

"It's okay," Gemma says, and we both take one arm up high, so it doesn't pop from the socket as we swing her.

"That was fun," Kaitlyn says as we reach the car. She hops into the back to buckle herself in, and I glance around to see what Gemma is driving.

"I walk to school," she says. "I bought a townhouse a few blocks away."

"Oh, nice. I didn't realize." I pull her door open for her.

"Ride me." What the fuck. I give a quick shake of my head at my blunder. "I mean ride *with* me," I say quickly.

"I know what you meant," she says, mature enough not to needle me as she slides into the car and sets her papers on the back seat beside Kaitlyn. None of the guys at the station would have let that go, and when I say guys, I mean the female fighters. I love them all dearly, like family, but they love to *ride* my ass—as in harass me relentlessly, all in good fun of course. I get a whiff of her scent as she settles in my passenger seat, and I tug my hair, closing the door behind her.

Ride me?

Really, Callan?

Shit, it was a simple slip, but now that I've said it, I kind of can't stop thinking about it. Me in bed, sweet Gemma on top of me. My dick twitches as I circle the car and I clench my teeth and work to purify my thoughts. Yeah, the guys are right. I do need to get laid. I never was the kind of guy to sleep around, but maybe it's time for a one-night stand. Not with Gemma, of course. We're just friends. Yeah, sure she was cute in high school, but four years of college later, combined with a couple years of teaching, well, let's just say she turned into a beautiful woman. I can't understand why she's still single. Maybe her break-up with Brad was recent, and she's not ready to get back into the game. I can understand that.

I back out of my spot and head toward Boston Common. Fifteen minutes later we're walking through the park, eating our dripping ice-cream cones. Joggers run the path around the park, as families picnic, or play with their pets.

"I'm going to teach Gilbert how to fetch," Kaitlyn states unambiguously, and Gemma stifles a chuckle when I glance at her.

"That'll be a neat trick," I say, and zero in on the big stain of ice cream on Gemma's face. "You have a bit..." I reach for her face, and she jerks backward. Whoa. What the hell? "Sorry, you just have some ice cream on your face."

"Right, okay," she says, her eyes big as she swipes her mouth with a napkin.

Fuck, I've been the first on the scene in many situations, including domestic abuse. If I didn't know better... Hell, I don't know better. A burst of protectiveness goes through me. "Everything okay, Gemma?"

"Yeah, sure," she says, all bright-eyed. "You just startled me." She turns her attention to Kaitlyn. "Will you be at the Boys and Girls club this summer?" she asks, and I don't miss the fast switch in conversations.

"Will I be, Daddy?"

"You bet you will be. But next week you're going to stay with Grammy and Grampy, remember?" I say, my stomach coiled tight. Is someone hurting Gemma? If so, I'd like to meet them, and introduce my fist to their face.

"Grammy has a bird," she says.

"What kind of bird?" Gemma asks.

Kaitlyn holds her hands a couple inches apart. "It's a perky." She rolls her eyes. "I like him but he sings a lot."

"Parakeet," I correct. In the distance I spot fellow fire-fighter Colin and the guys playing frisbee. I waved as we pass, and inside Gemma's purse her phone starts ringing—a ring-tone I don't recognize, which probably means its personalized and she knows who's calling. She tenses and ignores the chime. It keeps on ringing, the caller as tenacious as a six-year-old.

"You going to get that?" I ask.

"No," she says flatly.

I shove my hands into my pockets, and cast her a sidelong glance, aware of the tightness in her shoulders, her rapid intake of breath. "Want me to get it for you?"

"No, it's..." Her head slowly lifts, her eyes filled with something that looks like despair when they latch on mine.

I come to an abrupt halt. "Jesus, Gemma, what is it?"

***

If you want to see what kind of trouble Gemma and Callan get into, check it out here! **Single Dad Burning Up**

The Rule Breaker

In the Line of Duty

His Obsession Next Door

His Strings to Pull

His Trouble in Talulah

His Taste of Temptation

His Moment to Steal

His Best Friend's Girl

His Reason to Stay

Confessions

Confessions of a Bad Boy Professor

Confessions of a Bad Boy Officer

Confessions of a Bad Boy Fighter

Confessions of a Bad Boy Doctor

Confessions of a Bad Boy Gamer

Confessions of a Bad Boy Millionaire

Confessions of a Bad Boy Santa

Confessions of a Bad Boy CEO

Hands On

Hands On

Body Contact

Full Exposure

Dossier

Private Reserve

House Rules

Under Pressure

Big Catch

Brazilian Fantasy

Improper Proposal

Boys of Beachville

Good at Being Bad

Igniting the Bad Boy

Bad Girl Therapy

Stone Cliff Series:

Crashing Down

Wasted Summer

Love Lessons

Wrapped Up

Eternal Pleasure Series

Instinctive

Impulsive

Indulgent

Sun Stroked Series

Seaside Seduction

Deep Desire

Private Pleasure

Captured and Claimed Series:

Yours to Take

Yours to Teach

Yours to Keep

Firefighter Heat Series

Fever

Siren

Flash Fire

Playing For Keeps Series

Slow Ride

Wild Ride

Sweet Ride

Breaking the Rules:

Hold Me Down Hard

Pin Me Up Proper

Tie Me Down Tight

Stand Alone Title:

Hands on with the CEO

Torn Between Two Brothers

Holiday Spirit

Unleashed

Knocking on Demon's Door

Web of Desire

ABOUT CATHRYN

New York Times and *USA today* Bestselling author, Cathryn is a wife, mom, sister, daughter, and friend. She loves dogs, sunny weather, anything chocolate (she never says no to a brownie) pizza and red wine. She has two teenagers who keep her busy with their never ending activities, and a husband who is convinced he can turn her into a mixed martial arts fan. Cathryn can never find balance in her life, is always trying to find time to go to the gym, can never keep up with emails, Facebook or Twitter and tries to write page-turning books that her readers will love.

Connect with Cathryn:
Newsletter https://app.mailerlite.com/webforms/landing/c1f8n1
Twitter: https://twitter.com/writercatfox
Facebook: https://www.facebook.com/AuthorCathrynFox?ref=hl
Blog: http://cathrynfox.com/blog/
Goodreads: https://www.goodreads.com/author/show/91799.Cathryn_Fox

Pinterest http://www.pinterest.com/catkalen/

www.ingramcontent.com/pod-product-compliance
Lightning Source LLC
Chambersburg PA
CBHW021143190726
48288CB00008B/2802